# Power in Darkness

### Supernatural Community
### Book Two

## KRISTA STREET

# Also by Krista Street

For the most up-to-date list of Krista's books, visit her website: www.kristastreet.com

# Chapter 1

Thick black illness swirled into my palms. My hands hovered above my client's head, absorbing his sickness.

He lay quietly on my healing table with his eyes closed. Acne covered his cheeks, and wispy stubble grazed his chin. At nineteen, he'd only just begun adulthood.

Sweat beaded along my upper lip, and my palms trembled. In my client's mind, the diseased cells dipped and played, toying with me. They were trying to hide and evade my powerful internal light.

*You can't hide from me. I'll find you.*

Heat radiated from my palms as I sought every imbalance in his brain. Silence filled the small storage shed as I worked my light. Only the hard concrete floor beneath my soles registered in my mind. Everything else—the autumn wind rustling through the shed's thin walls, my client's anxious mother rocking in the corner, Cecile's intense gaze as she watched over the healing session—had faded.

I bit my lip as my hands shifted to my client's ears. My light flowed into his temporal lobes, and I grimaced. He had so many chemical imbalances—definitely schizophrenia.

A voice cackled to my left when I extracted a particularly diseased section, but I ignored it. I knew the voice wasn't real since my client's persistent hallucinations were transferring to me.

I worked deeper into my client's mind, encircling and capturing the demented cells.

*That's it. Almost done.*

When the last remnant of my client's mental illness transferred to me, I hunched over, my hands gripping the edge of the portable bed tightly. My harsh pants filled the room.

"You stupid, bitch! Do you really think you can beat me?" A haggard-looking old woman appeared on my left, stringy gray hair hanging around her shoulders. Her gnarled hands reached for me. "You think you're so smart, playing witch doctor with kids. You're no witch! You're a fake! No wonder your mother died. It was the only way to be rid of you!" She laughed, the sound ugly and twisted.

I squeezed my eyes shut and called up my light, pulling all of it from where I stored it deep below my navel. The hot fire climbed from my belly into my mind, burning me and the schizophrenia as it went. The cackling woman beside me faded, her voice growing quieter, as my healing light rid me of my client's hallucinations.

"What's she doing?" my client's mother asked, her voice quietly drifting to me from where she sat in the corner of the storage shed.

"Shh!" Cecile hissed. "Daria needs absolute quiet and concentration to work her gift."

I tuned them out and coaxed my light to burn stronger. Heat burst through my mind, destroying the last sick remnants in its path.

The haggard woman shattered into oblivion as my light shot from my fingertips in a powerful eruption, bathing the room in gold.

A muffled shriek came from my client's mother.

A moment passed, then another. Slowly, the sounds and smells of the small storage shed permeated my mind: soft cries of gratitude came from my client, the squeak of his mother's chair as she hurried forward to reach him, and scents of lavender and rosemary from the burning candles tickled my nose. Finally, Cecile's quiet footsteps tapped as she approached me from behind.

I stayed bent over the table, sweat dripping from my forehead. Fatigue rolled through my body, but already, it was passing.

Cecile squeezed my shoulder comfortingly but removed her hand just as my light rushed upward from my navel. The shocks that came from people touching me, activating my gift, never occurred during Cecile's brief affections. She was one of the few people that understood my touching limitations.

"We have ten minutes before your next client arrives. Is that enough time?"

I nodded and grabbed the small towel Cecile held out to me. I wiped the sweat from my brow before handing it back to her. Even though the temperature hovered around sixty-five, I felt hot and winded, as if I'd just run five miles.

"Thank you! Thank you for healing him!" my client's mother gushed.

She rushed forward and reached for my hand just as her son sat upright on the portable bed. He stared at me with a look of disbelief.

I let the mother squeeze my hand briefly but pulled back when a painful flare followed. "How are you feeling?" I asked her son.

He shook his head, a look of amazement on his face. "I feel fine. Really good, actually. The voices . . . they're gone."

I smiled warmly before Cecile ushered them out of the shed.

After grabbing my water bottle, I took a long drink then bit into a granola bar. I chewed quickly, knowing I didn't have much time. Sure enough, only a few minutes passed before a car door slammed. I chugged another drink and set my things down.

The door to the storage shed creaked open. In hobbled an elderly woman with her husband at her side. One of her legs was shorter than the other, her gait uneven. She'd been a victim of polio in her toddler years. Within half an hour, she would be free of the virus's destruction on her body—just as soon as my light burned away her sickness.

∞  ∞  ∞

That night, I lay on my bunk in our tour bus, twirling a strand of my blond hair around my finger, my phone pressed to my ear. Our ancient bus rumbled beneath me as Mike drove us to my next venue. Above my bed, through the narrow window, I could see the full moon. It lit up the sky.

"How did things go today?" I asked Logan, my former bodyguard and newly appointed boyfriend. He, along with his three werewolf friends—Jake, Alexander, and Brodie—were all in California, trying to track down someone who had stolen a dragon from a dragon trainer.

Logan grumbled. "Not good. The culprit knows how to cover his tracks. He's all but disappeared."

"So not an easy fix." I sighed.

I still couldn't believe that dragons existed and weren't just in fairytales and movies. The times Logan had spoken of the supernatural community during the past few days had only increased my desire to visit him. I bit my lip and let my hair fall before turning on my side.

"And how are your friends?" I asked.

Jake, Alexander, and Brodie were also members of the Supernatural Forces, the supernatural community's version of the armed guards and law enforcement combined. The four of them were in the same squad.

"Good, but their teasing me about you is getting irritating."

I laughed.

"So where's your next stop?" Logan asked.

I peeked out the window. Dark mountains surrounded us as we climbed a steep hill. "Not far from Bozeman—I think some small town north of I-90." I let the curtain fall. "It's hard to believe tomorrow's my last day off. That means my tour's almost finished." A delicious thrill ran through me at what *that* meant. Already, a week had passed since Logan boarded a Greyhound bus in Miles City. It had been a long week without him.

I expected Logan to come back with an excited remark, instead, his tone turned serious. "North of Bozeman? That's werewolf territory."

I perked up. "It is? Does that mean I'll run into other people from your pack?"

"Not likely in that area." He grumbled again, tension strumming along the line. "Be careful, and steer clear of any stray wolves, okay? You have no idea what kind of scent your magic gives off. Other wolves will know you're a supernatural, which to them means you're ripe for the picking."

I snickered. "I wouldn't even know how to steer clear of one. You all look like any other human, other than the fact that you're all freakishly huge."

Again, my teasing tone didn't alleviate his grave one. "We're all big, yes. That's the only clue you'll get if you meet one of us, but Dar, be mindful of who you run into. Okay? Having to contend with another wolf for you would be painful enough, but they're not who I'm worried about. I've heard rumors of a few rogues in that area."

"What are rogues?"

"They're wolves that have left packs and live alone, but any werewolf who's alone for an extended period of time changes. Packs keep us civil, more human than animal, but rogues . . ." He paused, and I would have sworn he was running his hand through his hair. "They're not like me or my friends. They're vicious and cruel, and if you encountered a rogue and resisted him, he'd most likely force himself on you."

"Really?" I shuddered. "Are rogues common? How many are there?"

"Less than a hundred that we know of, but that's a hundred too many. The SF is always trying to track down and capture them."

My stomach tightened, my teasing mood evaporating. "Okay, I'll be careful, but what do you mean about my scent? You can smell my magic? You've never mentioned that before."

He sighed heavily. "I still have so much to tell you, but yes, your magic has a scent. Witches have a floral smell. Your magic smells like blooming roses, and it's strong. In general, the stronger the magic, the stronger the scent."

A lightbulb clicked on inside me. *So that's what Alexander was talking about.* One of Logan's friends had made a comment about me smelling like roses when I'd overheard the four of them talking about me after a particularly brutal healing session the other week.

"And that part about me being ripe for the picking, what does that mean?"

"Supes are only allowed to date other supes, so you'll be seen as a potential mate by other wolves within the community."

I sat up, swinging my legs over my bunk. My long blond hair fell over my shoulders. "Wait, so supernaturals aren't allowed to date humans?"

"Not without special permission from the courts. The community's law changed about ten years ago. Some supes have dated humans in the past—like your mom—and some even married them, but not all marriages and relationships last, and when a jilted lover is looking for revenge, what better way to do that than to draw attention to us? We've had a few sticky situations when humans reported us to the government and other organizations that would benefit from having supes on their payrolls."

My feet thumped quietly on the floor when I hopped down from my bunk. I'd never been able to date humans because of my light, so that realization didn't particularly bother me. "I had no idea, but don't worry. I'll be careful. I won't run into any single werewolves looking for a girlfriend, and I'll try to avoid any rogues."

He chuckled. "Good. Avoid any and all single werewolves, cause I'm not the sharing type. You're mine, Daria Gresham, and mine alone."

Goose bumps tingled on my arms from the possessive growl in his tone. Next came the familiar tightening in my core when I pictured Logan's large hands running along my body as he showed me just how possessive he was. Already, dampness coated my panties. He'd made me react that way from day one.

Squirming, I was about to ask him more about dragons when Logan added quietly, "And, Dar? I mean it about the rogues. If you come across any—run."

∞  ∞  ∞

Logan's words sank in after we hung up, snuffing out some of the desire that burned in me. It was crazy to think I'd never encountered another werewolf or supernatural before, but Logan said I probably *had* but hadn't known it.

According to him, the community knew that my family had excommunicated themselves centuries ago—for what reason, I still didn't know—so most left us alone. But because word was out that I knew about the community and intended to visit, he didn't know if that would still be the case.

I bit my lip as I stood in the dressing room, looking for clean pajamas. With a flick of my fingers and a muttered spell under my breath, two sets of pajamas floated up from the drawer and hovered in front of me. I grabbed the blue pair—a skimpy tank top with matching shorts—and slipped them on.

Frowning, I mulled over what Logan had told me. Despite unquenched desire flowing through my veins—the result of hearing Logan's voice—his words also reminded me that we led separate lives, mine in the human world and his in the supernatural one.

*But it doesn't have to be that way.*

I chewed on my nail, my brow furrowing. Unbidden thoughts kept entering my mind, tempting me to walk away from my calling. But my supernatural healing tour waiting list was two years long. Sick people who were hoping to still be alive by the time their appointment arrived were counting on me. Yet as each day progressed and my life outside of the supernatural community continued, I began to question if I really wanted to continue my tours. Every day, our nomadic existence grew less and less appealing.

*But I'm a Gresham!*

I held on to that thought, trying to find comfort in it. After all, according to my ancestors, our gift was created to help others, to heal them.

And at the moment, I was the only Gresham woman in the world since my mother and my grandmother had died the previous year. If I didn't continue our way of life, if I didn't birth a daughter and raise her to do what we did, my family's legacy would die with me. Centuries of my people's sacrifices would have been for nothing.

I hung my head. My mom had told me that doubt would eventually plague me—that I would question my purpose in life, even want to abandon it. The path my ancestors had chosen wasn't easy. It required sacrifice. I knew all too well what she was referring to now.

The urge to stomp my foot and rail at my predicament grew almost uncontrollable with every passing mile as our bus rumbled down the interstate. Frustration over my life and longing for something that could never be had haunted me all week.

*Why couldn't I have been born a normal witch? One without these great expectations?*

Despite only a week passing since Logan had left,

already the distance was wearing on me, and even though I wanted to be with Logan, considering our current circumstances—my responsibility to my clients, and his to the SF—I didn't know if that was possible.

That was one reason why my mother and my nan had never married. Most in my family didn't. Our calling was to heal others, not to pursue a life of self-gratification.

Cecile nudged the door open. "Everything okay, Dar?"

Her perfect gray bun sat just above the nape of her neck. Whistling drifted down the aisle from the driver's seat. Mike had the radio cranked up.

I forced a smile and stood up straighter. "Yeah. Fine. Just thinking about something."

"Well, it's getting late." She checked her watch. "You may want to get to sleep since tomorrow is the only day you can sleep in before your tour finishes."

"Of course, good idea." I crammed the second pair of pajamas back in the drawer. "So after my show tomorrow, how much farther west are we going?"

"Western Washington is the last stop, just south of Seattle."

I took some comfort in that. Western Washington strayed well out of rogue territory. Once we hit that state and moved progressively west, fewer stray wolves would be around, and if less than a hundred werewolves had gone rogue from the community, the chances of me actually running into one were pretty small.

At least that was one worry I wouldn't have to think about.

# Chapter 2

"Have we got it all, Cece?" I pushed our heavy shopping cart toward one of the supermarket checkout lines. Around us, the steady *beep beep* of checkout scanners filled the air. Since it was my last day off, we were doing really exciting things—like grocery shopping.

Cecile held up her shopping list and checked things off with a pencil. "I think so. Those steaks should be delicious tonight. Mike will be excited that we splurged on them. We can even pull out the Weber and properly grill them. What do you think?" She set another item on the conveyer belt. "Dar?"

"What? Oh, yeah." I shook myself, trying to not let my increasing anxiety over what my future held get the better of me. All day, I'd had a hard time concentrating.

"Steaks sound good."

After paying, we wheeled the old cart into the parking lot. The rickety wheels spun noisily along the pavement as morning sunshine streamed down, and the Rockies loomed around us like giant bowling pins.

Once we reached the bus, Mike ambled down the steps to help us load everything. His bushy black hair brushed his shoulders, and his mustache tilted up with his smile when he saw the steaks.

"Now that's the kind of meal I'm talking about!" He pulled his Yankees cap down more when the sun reached his eyes.

We carried everything onto the bus and began unloading.

I cursed under my breath when the empty coffee canister on the counter caught my attention. "I forgot the coffee."

"You did?" Cecile's arm paused in midair, a box of pasta in her hand. "But I thought you grabbed it."

Mike brought a hand to his heart in mock pain. "Well, we certainly can't live without coffee. One of us had better run back and get it."

"I'll go. It's my fault. I meant to grab it, but . . ." I'd been too caught up in mulling over Logan's and my future that I'd completely forgotten why I was standing in the coffee aisle and had returned to shopping with Cece empty handed.

"Do you have enough money?" Mike asked.

"I think so." I dug around in my purse to make sure and pulled out a crumpled bill. Only ten bucks to my name at the moment. Payday couldn't come fast enough, *if* it came. We were still waiting on payment from a few clients. "Be right back."

After hopping down the bus's steps, I sprinted back to the store, my flip-flops slapping on the pavement. Since I didn't have my hair pulled back, my long blond locks flew around my shoulders as the warm September air swirled around my bare legs. I pushed through the doors, the air conditioning assaulting me, before jogging toward the coffee aisle and rounding the corner.

"Oh!" I collided with a hard chest, and the force was so great that I ricocheted off him and fell backward, landing unceremoniously on my butt in the middle of the store. Cool linoleum touched my fingertips when my hands splayed back to support me. My fall happened so fast, that for a moment, I sat there speechless.

"Oh shit!" A guy crouched at my side. "Are you okay? I'm sorry, I didn't see you." Genuine concern filled his voice.

I brought a shaky hand to my forehead as my cheeks flushed with embarrassment. "No, it's my fault. I was running and not watching where I was going. I didn't see you."

"Let me help you up."

He offered me his hand, but I inched back. The last thing I needed was an electric jolt from a stranger's touch. "It's okay. I'm fine." I pushed to stand and dusted my jean shorts off. *How embarrassing!*

The guy put his hands on his hips, and for the first time, I actually looked at him.

My eyes widened as they traveled up his frame—his very *large* frame.

He had to be at least six-four and had hazel eyes, sandy-brown hair, a firm mouth, and a square jaw. He looked young, not much older than my twenty-one years, and all of him was heavily muscled, reminding me of a certain group I'd said goodbye to not too long ago.

My breath caught in my throat. I took a step back, remembering Logan's warning. I had no idea if the guy was a werewolf, but if he was, I wouldn't have been surprised.

A crooked smile lifted his lips. He either hadn't picked up on my sudden wariness or had chosen to ignore it. "Are you all right? Not dizzy or anything?" Even though his gaze scanned my frame, I still caught the teasing in his tone.

I sighed inwardly and avoided the urge to roll my eyes at my paranoia. He was probably just another dude off the street who just happened to have a large build. It wasn't like being tall and muscled was *that* uncommon, and not every large male in the world was a werewolf.

A shaky, self-conscious laugh spilled from my lips as I forced myself to not take another step back. "No, I'm fine. Thanks for asking, though, and sorry again that I ran into you."

He shrugged. "Don't worry about it."

I smiled and stepped around him. When I brushed past him, his nostrils flared, just the barest hint.

*Paranoid, Dar! Stop being paranoid!*

Inwardly, I cursed Logan for putting me on edge for every male within a two-hundred-mile radius. Whether it was werewolf territory or not, most guys in the area were one hundred percent human.

My flip-flops slapped on the linoleum as I headed down the aisle. I grabbed the first can of coffee I saw. It was a generic brand, but it would do.

"You're not serious about drinking that, are you?"

The teasing question came from behind me. I turned around to see the same guy again. Apparently, he hadn't carried on shopping.

He picked up a different coffee can, a pretty picture of Columbian mountains on the label. "This stuff is a lot better and is almost the same price. Now, I'm not telling you what to buy, but trust me—I've tried every coffee in this place, and you definitely don't want to buy *that* one."

I propped my free hand on my hip. "Is that right?"

"Yeah, that stuff will put you in an early grave." His hazel eyes twinkled, but his nostrils flared again when he inhaled.

I reshelved the death-inducing coffee and took the one from his outstretched hand. "Okay, well, thank you." I skipped around him, heading toward the front of the store.

A second later, heavy steps came from behind me. As I rounded the corner, the guy fell into step beside me.

"And one more thing, I just want to put out the disclaimer that I'm not responsible if you don't like that coffee."

I stepped in line at the first checkout aisle and turned toward him, hand on my hip again. Maybe I *was* being paranoid, but he was really persistent on keeping our conversation going. "Are you following me?"

He made a horrified face. "Following you? Oh shit, is that how it seems?"

"Honestly, yeah, a little." The cash register beeped behind us as the checkout girl chatted easily with the woman ahead of me, but I kept my attention on the coffee connoisseur.

He cupped the back of his neck, a sheepish expression filling his face. "Can you tell I don't usually do this? I'm trying to strike up a conversation with you as best I can, and you think I'm following you." He shrugged and gave an exaggerated sigh. "And this is probably why I'm single."

I muffled a laugh, and for the first time since meeting him felt truly relaxed. *See, Dar. You're totally being paranoid. He's just a dude trying to get your number and seems genuinely mortified that you just called him out.*

He straightened, a smile stretching across his face when my lips quirked up. "So as I was saying, I hope that coffee will do."

I set the coffee on the conveyor belt since the woman ahead of me was pulling out her wallet. "Honestly, as long as it has caffeine, we're good."

"Not a picky lady. I like that."

My cheeks flushed at his blatant come-on. To cover it up, I picked up a magazine on the rack and leafed through it, but the huge, hazel-eyed, sandy-brown-haired guy, that—who was I kidding—was drop-dead gorgeous, made no attempts to leave.

"I never thought they'd stay together." His breath brushed against my ear, and I jumped. He pointed at the couple on the magazine's cover. "Even though I loved her in that one romantic comedy. You know the one— where the guy flies across the country three times to see her, but they keep missing each other, so don't actually meet until the end—or whatever?" He shrugged. "Even though in the movie, she's sweet, I think in real life, she's a bit of a psycho."

He said it so casually and nonchalantly that for the second time, I had the urge to laugh. When a chuckle escaped me, he grinned.

"She might be." I put the magazine back on the shelf and rummaged around in my purse for my crumpled ten-dollar bill since the woman ahead of me had just picked up her bags.

The guy took a step closer, his head cocking. "I can't help but notice that you're not from around here."

My hand stilled. "What makes you say that?"

"It's a small town. If someone like you had moved to town, I would know."

"What does *that* mean?"

He held up his hands in surrender, his eyes wide, then laughed. "Nothing bad! I swear. It's just that . . . you know." He shrugged and gave me a look as if I should know what he was talking about.

I raised an eyebrow. "I know . . . what?"

"That you're . . ." He ran a hand over the back of his neck again before dropping his gaze and muttering under his breath. Straightening, he said, "Look, I'm not very good at this pickup stuff, and it's been a while since I've done this, but you're drop-dead gorgeous, so I'd obviously have paid attention if you'd moved to town."

My mouth went dry. "Oh, I'm—"

"Miss? Is the coffee all you're getting?"

The checkout girl's voice made my attention snap to

her. I fumbled around in my purse again but dropped my wallet in the process. "Crap!" I bent down to get it at the same time the guy did. Our heads collided.

"Ouch!" I brought a hand to my forehead just as he winced.

"Shit! I'm sorry. Damn, that's the second time I've almost knocked you out. Trust me, this is *not* going as I intended it."

Since he seemed genuinely embarrassed, I gave him a sympathetic smile. "It's okay. Besides, I thought we agreed that our first collision was my fault."

He smiled. "Not only are you not picky about coffee, but you also don't blame a guy for everything that goes wrong. You're getting better and better by the second."

My cheeks had to be bright red by the time I stood and turned back to the checkout girl. She just snapped her gum, looking bored.

"That will be ten forty-eight." She held her hand out.

*Shit.* I hoped I had some change. Being careful, I retrieved my wallet and had the change clasp halfway open when the charmer beside me reached into his back pocket.

"I got it. Don't worry about it. This way, if you don't like the coffee, I won't feel bad."

"What? No! You don't have to—"

But he'd already shoved a twenty-dollar bill into the girl's outstretched hand, and before I could protest again, he was grabbing the receipt, his change, and the canister of coffee. He shoved the can under his arm, his bicep flexing.

"Can I walk you to your car?"

For the first time since encountering him, I looked around in confusion. "But aren't you shopping? Didn't you leave your cart somewhere or something?"

I stared at his empty hands, not counting my newly acquired coffee.

He just grinned. "I'll come back and get what I need after I walk you out. I figure if I get another few minutes with you, I can awkwardly ask for your number at least two times, in which you'll probably decline, but hey, can't blame a guy for trying."

"I can handle it. Really." I scrunched my nose up, guilt filling me since he was trying so hard. "And I have a boyfriend, so yeah, I would be turning you down." I bit my lip after that admission just as he brought a hand to his chest.

"Ouch. That one hurts. I guess I shouldn't be surprised, though. How can a girl like you be single?"

*If you only knew.* "But . . . thanks for the coffee." I held out my hands for the canister. "Are you sure I can't pay you back?"

He handed it over and shook his head. "No, it's on me, seriously. It was a pleasure meeting you . . ." He let the last words hang before holding his hand out.

I knew this was where I was supposed to shake his hand and tell him my name. After all he'd done, exchanging names wasn't asking too much. I drew in a quick breath to prepare myself for what was to come, then I placed my hand into his and said in a rush, "Daria."

His large palm closed over mine. I made a move to pull my hand back. My light was still in my internal storage box, but I cringed, waiting for the electric jolts and uncomfortable tingles.

They didn't come.

Instead, a warm rush flowed through my blood as my light stayed calmed. My eyes snapped wide open.

"Daria. That's a beautiful name." He continued to shake my hand as pleasant, soothing sensations tingled along my nerves. "I'm Jayden." He still held my hand, and the delicious sensations coursed up my arm. "Well, Daria, it was a pleasure to meet you." With that, he let go and turned on his heel.

I didn't move. I couldn't.

I just stared after him, my jaw dropping. Because for the second time that month, I'd met another potential mate.

# Chapter 3

*How the hell is this happening? First Logan, and now Jayden? What are the chances?*

I stumbled in a daze across the parking lot, still reeling from the encounter. Two eligible mates had entered my life in the past two weeks. That was unheard of. I couldn't remember ever meeting *one*.

But Mom had warned me that could happen. As I matured and grew, my gift would begin to search for a mate. I was old enough to birth my sole daughter and care for her, so I shouldn't be that surprised that I had met two guys back to back.

*Even so . . . WTF?*

My senses still tingled from the encounter. Thank god my nipples were under control.

Logan's face flashed through my mind as I walked to the bus door. Guilt followed. I'd just had a purely physical reaction to a man I didn't even know. What did that say about me?

I closed my eyes and pictured my former bodyguard. His six-foot-three, hot-as-hell body filled my mind. I remembered his shoulders. They were so broad that they usually brushed doorways when he passed through them. Thick dark hair covered his head. His complexion was unblemished, his features chiseled, and in a nutshell, he was absolutely mouthwatering.

Opening my eyes, I continued to sail toward the bus.

I missed Logan—terribly. And it wasn't just my body's reaction to him that I missed—I wasn't that shallow. I also missed *him*. I missed his company and soothing presence. I missed how easy he was to talk to and the sound of his laugh. I missed his chivalrous, doting behavior.

I missed everything about him.

So even though my body recognized Jayden as another potential mate, my heart didn't. I still wanted Logan. Only Logan.

*Still . . .*

"Unbelievable," I whispered.

"There you are!" Cecile exclaimed when I climbed aboard. "I was just about to send Mike out looking for you."

A fierce blush stained my cheeks when I set the coffee on the counter. "Sorry. I didn't mean to take so long."

Cecile cocked her head. She sat on the couch, her

astute gaze scanning my pink cheeks. "We're going to stop at that park we saw on our way into town. Does a picnic lunch sound okay?"

I threaded a hand self-consciously through my hair. "Yeah. Sure. That's fine."

She raised her eyebrows just as Mike started the bus. The low rumble vibrated beneath my soles.

"Here we go!" he called.

I stumbled to the back of the bus as he turned out of the parking lot. I could feel Cecile's gaze follow me and knew if I stayed in the front, she would keep pressing me to tell her what was wrong. But at the moment, I just couldn't.

∞  ∞  ∞

"Dar, are you sure you're okay?" Logan's deep voice strummed through the phone.

It was the third time he'd asked me that question, and we'd only been on the phone for ten minutes. It was only four in the afternoon in California, so he was still working, but I'd needed to hear his voice, so I'd called anyway, breaking our normal routine of only phoning in the evenings.

"I'm fine," I replied too quickly.

My leg fidgeted as I sat on a picnic bench and bit my lip. We'd parked the bus near the park Cecile had spotted earlier. Since the park was close to the edge of town, there weren't strict parking restrictions. We intended to spend the night.

Logan grumbled. "It's pretty obvious you're not fine.

I don't think you've ever called me in the middle of the day then proceeded to barely say three words." His voice softened. "Do you want to talk about it?"

My foot jiggled more as I chewed my fingernail. Before I could lose my nerve, I blurted, "I met another potential mate at the grocery store this morning, and it's kinda freaking me out!"

I breathed heavily, waiting for his reaction.

It didn't come.

"Logan?"

Another few seconds passed before he asked in a strained voice, "Did you say potential *mate*?"

I cringed. "Yeah, but it's not what you think. I just don't know how else to describe it. My mom warned me about this. It's part of our magic that when we're of age, our bodies start searching for mates, and before you, I hadn't met anyone whose touch I could handle, but now, it's happened again." I rubbed my free hand over my jean shorts. My palms suddenly felt clammy.

"So, what exactly happened?"

I could have sworn he'd just stood and started pacing.

"I ran into a guy at the grocery store this morning, and I fell over. Like literally *fell over* cause I ran right into him. Then he helped me pick out coffee and started following me, but in a nice way, not a creepy way, then at the checkout counter he shook my hand goodbye, and that's when I realized his touch didn't bother me, not like most people, and I don't know . . . it was weird, but there you have it."

I paused to take a breath because I was damned near hyperventilating.

But Logan stayed quiet.

Rubbing my free hand against my shorts again, I added, "But it doesn't change how I feel about you. I still like you, *only* you, but it was weird. The guy was huge, similar to you, Jake, Alexander, and Brodie, so I immediately thought he might be a werewolf, but I think he's really just a guy my body recognized as another potential mate. So anyway, that's why I called. I needed to hear your voice, and I don't know—get it off my chest or something, and I really just . . . well, I don't know."

I cringed again. *For fuck sake, stop talking, Dar!*

But only his silence followed.

"Logan? Say something. You told me to tell you what was bothering me, so I did." My entire calf was wiggling. If he didn't reply, I would be pacing the park soon.

A sound finally came from his end—an audible swallow. "So . . . let me get this straight," he said in that strained-sounding voice. "You met a guy who *touched* you, and you . . . what? Liked it? Got turned on by it? I'm trying to understand here, Dar. Help me out."

"No! Not turned on. It was just . . . his touch was bearable and soothing, kind of like yours. That's how I knew he was another potential mate."

"His touch was like mine . . ."

"No, not like yours! I mean, I didn't want to jump his bones or anything, and my nipples didn't harden—"

*"What?"*

I slapped a hand to my forehead. *Freakin' A, Dar!* "Never mind. Ignore that comment about my nipples. It's kind of an inside joke with myself."

A commotion sounded in the background, as if

Logan was not only pacing, but also kicking things as he went.

"Logan?"

He growled, an actual growl. *Double, triple, and quadruple crap!* Our conversation was going worse than I'd thought it would.

"So, to recap," he said, "you met another guy, possibly a werewolf, who you're attracted to, and your body says you'd be happy to mate with him, and you know this all because he touched you long enough for you to feel that, and—"

"No!" I cut him off before biting my lip. "Well . . . yes. But it doesn't work like that. I still choose. Meeting him just means my body recognized him as a mate. It doesn't mean I *choose* him as a mate. You see? Big difference. And I still choose you."

"But he was following you?" The commotion from his end finally stopped. "Was he persistent? Did he try to force himself on you?"

"No, nothing like that. He just asked for my number, but I told him I had a boyfriend."

"Fuck me," Logan whispered. "I leave you alone for one week, and another dude is already trying to take my place, and he may be another motherfucking werewolf on top of it."

Okay. He was pissed. Seriously pissed. But honestly, how did I think this was going to go? "Logan, you don't need to worry. I don't want him. I still only want you."

Another grumble came from his end. "Where are you?"

I looked around. A grove of trees swayed at the end

of the park, and a swing set waited on the other side of the picnic area. "Um . . . in a park."

"What park? What city? And did you get the guy's name?"

"I don't know the park's name, but we're in Silver City in western Montana, and the guy's name is Jayden, but I don't know his last name."

"I'm going to check the database for a werewolf named Jayden, and Dar? If Jayden shows up again . . ." He growled. "Fuck. I know I can't order you around and tell you what to do, but every instinct in me is telling me to claim you right now and to keep you the hell away from him."

"Claim me?" My breath stopped at the sheer possessiveness of his tone. Logan had told me about claiming before, and it sounded pretty intense.

"Just don't go anywhere, okay?" he added. "I'm taking the next flight out and coming to you."

"What about your job and the dragon problem?"

"That can wait. You're more important."

∞  ∞  ∞

Grass brushed along the sides of my feet as I paced the park. An hour had passed since my conversation with Logan. I'd texted him a few times but had gotten no reply. I didn't know if that meant he was on a plane with his phone off or something came up at work and he couldn't leave after all.

Whatever the case, anxiety rolled through me like a pounding ocean surf.

My flip-flops slapped against my heels as I nibbled my fingernail. The bus lay behind me on the other side of the park, barely visible through the trees, but that was fine with me. I needed to keep moving so I could think.

Logan was coming because he was freaking out about another guy.

Even though he didn't need to worry about Jayden, a thrilling tingle ran down my spine. I had no idea how long it would take him to arrive from California, but one way or another, hopefully I would see him soon.

I was grinning when I reached the end of the park. A playground and a picnic area filled the lawn back by the bus, but at the end where I'd ventured, trees surrounded the perimeter.

I inhaled the fresh air, goose bumps rising along my arms since evening had set in. With it, came cooler temps.

"We meet again," someone with a deep voice said.

I shrieked and whirled around.

Jayden leaned nonchalantly against a tree, his arms crossed over his bare chest. Sweat dripped down his rock-hard abs as he smiled at me. My gaze briefly traveled up and down his frame. I couldn't help it. He only wore shorts, and with his pose and sweaty muscles, he could have been a model for a shirtless-man calendar.

"I thought that was you." He pushed away from the tree and walked slowly toward me.

I jumped back. "Jayden? What the hell! Are you following me?"

He stopped, his eyes growing wide. "What? No!" He raised his hands. "Honestly, no, I'm not. This just happens to be a park I run in a lot, and I caught your—"

He averted his gaze. "I, uh . . . I thought it was you over here."

*Caught my* . . . I fought the urge to roll my eyes. I would bet a million dollars he was about to say that he'd caught my scent, which meant he was definitely a werewolf. I studied him. He had stopped advancing the moment I'd grown wary, and he didn't seem intent on closing the gap between us.

All of my instincts were telling me he was a good guy. He wasn't like my father, Dillon Parker, but he was a werewolf, and Logan said to be cautious of them.

I took a deep breath then blurted, "Do I smell like roses?"

His dejected expression disappeared. He straightened and smiled, his hazel eyes warming. "Yeah, actually, you do."

I crossed my arms, and that time I *did* roll my eyes, not even trying to hide it. *He's totally a werewolf.* Logan was right. Apparently, more of them were around western Montana, but unlike what Logan had warned me about, Jayden didn't seem aggressive or like the rogues he'd been worried about. So far, Jayden had been nothing but polite. He was obviously just a normal werewolf.

*Might as well get it out in the open.* "So you're a werewolf?"

His smile grew. "You can tell? I wasn't sure if you could, and you're a witch, right? It's been a while since I've met a new supe, but your scent in the grocery store gave it away."

"As I've recently come to learn," I muttered under my breath.

His eyebrows knit together. "What was that?"

"Nothing." My arms dropped as I cocked my head. "Did you just shift recently? Is that what you do at this park? Go for runs in your wolf form?"

The happiness on his face was growing a mile a minute. "That's exactly right. This park is one of the few places in town where I can run close to home since the trees are so dense. Otherwise, I head out into the mountains, but that's only if I can stay in my wolf form for a couple of days."

"So are there other werewolves around here or just you?"

"There are three of us. We all share a house."

The sun dipped lower in the sky, making shadows appear around us, and my shoulders relaxed even more at how open he was being, especially since he lived with two other wolves. *Definitely not a rogue.* "So . . . are you guys part of the community?"

"Yeah, we're part of the community."

With every second that passed, I breathed easier. I glanced toward the bus. In the distance, Mike and Cecile were visible. They'd pulled out lawn chairs and, from the looks of it, had the grill going. Smoke rose from it.

"I should probably get back." I nodded toward them. "We're going to have dinner soon."

His gaze followed mine. "Are you camping over there?"

"Kind of but not really." I waved a hand at Cecile and Mike. "We live together in that bus and plan to spend the night here, but it will be in a bed, not a tent."

His eyes returned to mine then widened more. "Hang

on a minute. You're *that* Daria? Daria Gresham, the healing witch who travels on a bus?"

I stuffed my hands into my back pockets. "Um, yep. That's me. So you've heard of me?"

Jayden grinned, a full-on mega-watt-take-my-breath-away type of grin. "Of course I've heard of you. *Everyone's* heard of you. But I thought you didn't know about the community, that your family excommunicated themselves a long time ago or something."

I ran a hand through my hair. *So the entire community does know about me. Yeah, not weird at all.* "Ah, yeah. It's something like that, but I'm not in the dark anymore."

"Holy shit. I had no idea. It's an honor to meet you." He held his hand out again, as if we hadn't met before.

I reluctantly took it. As before, my light didn't respond. Instead, shivers ran through my entire body. *Okay, there's no point denying it. Logan's right—I'm attracted to Jayden. But that's merely my body talking. That's not my heart.*

Still, the realization was unsettling. In a way, it felt as if I had no control over myself. And although Jayden seemed like a nice, laid-back guy who was, let's face it, easy on the eyes, my stomach didn't flip with him. Not like it had when Logan and I first met.

I pulled my hand away and stuffed it awkwardly into my jeans pocket. "Well . . . nice seeing you again. I better get back."

"Oh, sure." His eyes dimmed when I turned toward the bus. "Hey, Daria? Any chance the three of you would like some company tonight? I could grab my pack mates, and we could come down here to join you guys. I bought potato salad and burgers at the grocery store today. We could grill the burgers and maybe have a beer or two?"

The hopeful tone of his voice made me bite back a smile. "So you *did* buy groceries today?"

He gave a crooked smile in return as a lock of sandy-brown hair fell across his forehead. "Yeah, believe it or not, I actually do buy groceries when I go to the supermarket. I don't just hit on pretty ladies."

I felt thankful for the falling sun. Otherwise, he would have seen my blush. "Well, I mean, I suppose if you all want to join us, that's fine."

I shifted my weight from foot to foot, trying to imagine how Logan would feel if he pulled up and I was having dinner with three werewolves.

*On second thought* . . . I was about to tell Jayden that maybe it *wasn't* a good idea when his crooked smile grew.

"Let me run home and grab the guys. We'll be back in twenty minutes. That cool?"

I smiled weakly, not having the heart to tell him no since he looked so excited. "Yeah, totally fine."

His smile was so wide that I cringed. I was fine with welcoming his company, along with his friends, but I didn't want more than that. Hopefully, I wouldn't need to spell it out for him.

After all, he knew I had a boyfriend. So everything would be fine. *Right?*

# Chapter 4

"You invited three werewolves to join us?" Mike crouched near the front of the bus. The small Weber sat at his feet, the coals heating.

I coughed and swished the smoke away that swirled in my eyes. "Technically, he invited himself and his friends."

"How the heck did you find three new werewolves in the eight hours we've been here?" Mike's eyes twinkled. "Have you become a wolf magnet?"

*If you only knew.*

I hadn't shared with Mike and Cecile some of the new things I'd learned about myself. As humans, they couldn't detect my magical rosy scent, but I had a feeling that very scent had been why Jayden had followed me in the supermarket. Logan certainly found my fragrance appealing.

I furrowed my brow when I checked my phone again. Still no text from my former bodyguard. My heart sank. I thought for sure Logan would have texted if he was about to board a plane or to let me know when he would arrive. *He must have been held up at work.* Perhaps he wasn't coming after all.

Shoulders slumping, I was about to climb aboard the bus to help Cecile carry the steaks and condiments outside when Jayden and two other large guys rounded the front fender. My eyes widened, and I stopped in my tracks. They'd approached silently—like predators.

Jayden smiled when he saw me, his eyelids hooded. The two dudes behind him appraised me up and down, their nostrils flaring.

"Oh, hi." Nervously, I ran a hand through my hair. I had no idea how strong my magical scent was, but considering every werewolf around me was constantly sniffing, I figured it was pretty strong.

I forced myself to stop fidgeting and shoved my hands into the back pockets of my jeans. My breasts jutted out.

All three guys' gazes dipped.

I hastily withdrew my hands and crossed my arms over my chest.

Jayden returned to planet Earth first. He shook himself, his gaze leaving my boobs. "Daria, these are my friends Niles and Zach." He waved at the two guys behind him.

The guy on the left, Zach, was shorter, probably around six feet, with blond hair and was built like a tank.

He lifted his chin. "What's up?"

I somehow managed a smile. "Not much. It's nice to meet you."

Jayden's other friend, Niles, continued to stare at me intently. He was the tallest of the three, probably six-six, with a leaner build and sinewy muscles.

I gave him a hesitant nod. "Hello."

"Hey."

Mike set his tongs down and wiped his hands on a towel. "Nice to meet you, fellas. I'm Mike." He held out his hand.

Jayden readily took it, followed by Zach then Niles.

I kept my arms crossed, still aware of their appreciative glances my way, just as Cecile hopped down the steps from the bus, awkwardly carrying the ketchup, mustard, buns, and a large bowl of cut-up watermelon.

"Oh!" She rushed to set the food down on the picnic table before she returned and smiled brightly at the newcomers. "You must be the three friends Daria said were coming to dinner. I'm Cecile."

"Nice to meet you, Cecile. I'm Jayden, and these two are Niles and Zach."

In her usual fashion, Cecile bestowed each of them with a serene smile and a gentle handshake.

With the introductions finished, Jayden held up the bag he carried. "I brought burgers and potato salad, just like I promised." He winked at me. "And plenty of beer for everyone." His other hand held a cooler.

Some of my self-consciousness over my ever-attention-demanding boobs dissipated. "Thanks, Jayden. I can take the potato salad."

"And I'll take those burgers." Mike reached forward. "I was just about to put the steaks on. I'll throw these on too."

"I cut up a watermelon, so this along with your potato salad means there should be plenty of food." Cecile bustled over to the picnic table. "Why don't you all have a seat?"

Mike straightened his Yankees cap before nodding toward the table. "Yeah, fellas, have a seat. I'll grill these up then we can eat."

Jayden sidled up to me as we walked the short distance to the table, his arm occasionally brushing against mine.

I put a few extra inches of distance between us, even though my senses didn't respond to him. I had a boyfriend, after all.

"It's pretty quiet around here," I commented. I'd only seen a few people venture to the park in the eight hours we'd been there. Nobody lingered around at the moment. "Is it always this quiet?"

"Usually. That's what I like about it and another one of the reasons I run here."

Behind us followed his two friends. I could feel them, their large, silent forms creating an energy of their own.

"I hope you're hungry," Cecile said as she set out paper plates and plastic silverware. "I also made a cake for dessert, so save room for that." She waved at the picnic table and surrounding lawn chairs, telling everyone to sit, before she started arranging the napkins. "Now, Daria tells me that you all live around here. How long have you been in the area?"

Jayden deposited the cooler on the ground before opening the lid. "The three of us have lived here for a few years now, and from what I hear, you and Mike travel with Daria?"

Cecile combed back the hair that had escaped her bun. "That's right. Mike and I have been with Daria since she was a little girl."

I settled on a lawn chair near the picnic table, and Jayden took the lawn chair beside me. He scooted the cooler closer to him and pulled out some beers.

Niles and Zach sat opposite one another at the end of the picnic table. The old wooden bench squeaked when Niles shifted to face me.

Jayden threw two beers to his friends in an impossibly fast move. My eyes widened as the beers sailed through the air. I was certain they would fly right past the two wolves. But when the beer flew in his direction, Niles's hand shot up and caught it in midair. His gaze never left my face.

My jaw dropped.

He smirked and winked.

With heated cheeks, I leaned back in my lawn chair and let out the breath I'd been holding. Werewolves moved *so* freakin' fast. Despite being with Logan and seeing him move like that, too, I still wasn't used to it.

"So how long are you guys planning to stay here?" Zach asked.

"Not long," I replied. "We'll have to leave tomorrow for my next show."

Jayden frowned. "Is it far?"

"A few hours," Cecile answered for me.

"So not so far that we couldn't meet up again?" Jayden asked cheekily.

"Um . . ." My cheeks had to be bright red by now.

I was thankful when Mike strolled up to the picnic table with a plate of steaks and saved me from having to reply. "I hope medium rare's okay," he said.

"That'll do," Jayden replied good-naturedly.

Zach helped himself to another beer, grabbing a second for Niles, too, before helping Mike set the food out.

Everyone helped themselves to the food, the scent of grilled meat and sweet watermelon filling the air.

When my stomach grumbled, Jayden nudged me playfully. "Hungry?"

I shrugged, then laughed uncomfortably. "Is it that obvious?"

"Nothing to be embarrassed about. I like a woman who can eat."

*Okay then . . .* I didn't know how to respond to that.

Everyone sat, and Mike soon busted out the latest baseball stats for the season. Since Jayden, Niles, and Zach all joined in the conversation, I figured they watched the sport too.

I added a few comments here and there, but considering baseball wasn't really my thing, I instead ate my food and sipped my beer.

The evening passed quickly once I got over how uncomfortable I felt. Jayden and his friends proved to be good company and easy to talk to and laugh with.

By the time twilight set in, I was sad to see them go, but I had a show the next day and needed a good night's rest. The coming week, as I finished up my tour, would prove grueling. Besides, even though I hadn't heard from Logan again, it was possible he was still coming. As for *when*, I still didn't know.

I pulled my cell phone from my pocket, hoping for a message from him.

Jayden's face dipped into shadows when he leaned my way. "Everything okay?"

I smiled sheepishly. It was the third time I'd checked my phone in fifteen minutes. "Yeah. Everything's fine. I'm just waiting to hear from somebody."

"Your boyfriend?"

I nodded. "I thought he would have texted by now."

Jayden leaned back in his chair and propped his elbow over the back of it. "What's your boyfriend's name? If you don't mind my asking."

I tucked a strand of hair behind my ears as the evening air swirled around, thankful that the smoky smell from the grill had died down. Nighttime scents had taken its place along with the sound of chirping crickets. "His name's Logan Smith. He's a werewolf too."

"Logan Smith?" Niles's head shot up. "Did you say Logan Smith?"

"Yeah."

Niles and Zach shared looks.

In the darkening night, I couldn't decipher it, but I watched the exchange with raised eyebrows. "Do you know him?"

"No, we don't know him," Jayden cut in. "But everybody knows *of* him. Logan is pretty well-known in the werewolf community."

I figured that was because Logan was in the Supernatural Forces, or SF. "Oh, right. That makes sense."

"Well, it's starting to get late," Cecile said as she began to collect the dishes. "And Daria has to work tomorrow, so we might have to head in, but it was a pleasure to meet you all."

They all mumbled in agreement.

I slipped my phone out of my pocket and glanced at it one more time. Still no messages. *Where is he?*

"Daria?" Cecile asked. "Do you mind helping?"

When Cecile handed me the condiments, I hastily set my phone on the table.

Mike stood and tipped his Yankees cap in the werewolves' direction. "Nice to meet you, fellas. I'm gonna go clean up the grill."

"Let me help you." Zach joined Mike.

"I'll be right back," I said to Jayden and Niles before following Cecile into the bus.

"You need any help?" Jayden asked.

"Nah. We got it."

Inside, Cecile clicked the lights on before we put the refrigerated items away. I filled the sink with hot, soapy water, and Cecile set to work on the dishes.

"I'll just tell them all goodnight then will be in."

Cecile dipped her hands into the suds. "Take your time."

I jogged back outside to collect the remaining items and say goodbye to my new friends. My phone was still on the picnic table. I glanced at it again before slipping it into my pocket. *Ugh.* Still nothing.

Zach had returned from helping Mike, and Niles and Jayden seemed ready to go.

I shoved my hands into my pockets. "Thanks for stopping by. I hope you guys have a good weekend."

Jayden's shoulders fell. "I guess this is goodbye then."

"I know it's not that late, but Cecile's right. I have to work tomorrow, so we're turning in. It was nice to meet you, though."

Despite the darkening sky, I still caught Jayden's growing frown.

He pulled me to the side. As before, his touch didn't aggravate my light. "So . . . I don't expect you to take me up on this, but if you're ever in the area again, do you want to look me up?" He handed over a piece of paper with his phone number on it.

I took it, but in the dark, I couldn't make out the number. Logan would *not* be thrilled at me collecting numbers from random guys, but Jayden had been polite and civil ever since I'd met him . . . if a little flirty. "Sure. I'll let you know if I'm ever back here."

Banging came from behind the bus as Mike locked the under-bus storage compartment. "I'm locking up, Dar. You coming?"

I nodded. "Coming!" I turned back to Jayden. "See you later?"

Jayden smiled. "I hope so."

"Bye," I said to his friends. "Have a good night."

They waved their goodbyes, and I turned away.

Once we'd stepped on board, Mike locked the bus up for the night, and the three of us got ready for bed. As I was brushing my teeth in the bathroom, my phone vibrated. I pulled it from my pocket to see a text from a strange number.

Cocking my head, I quickly finished brushing my teeth then opened it.

*Hey, babe. I'm in Montana. Sorry for not getting in touch sooner. I lost my phone in the airport in California. I swear the TSA stole it, so this is my new number. I'm at the park you said you were at. Where are you? I can't find you, but I'm on the west side.*

A grin spread across my face as I hastily tapped in a reply. No wonder I hadn't heard from Logan. *We're in the bus, just getting ready for bed, but I'm still dressed. Do you want me to find you since you can't find us?*

*Sure. I'm in a parking lot by a bunch of trees. Any chance you know what I'm talking about?*

My smile grew broader as tingles of excitement grew in my belly. I knew exactly where he was talking about. That was near the area where I'd run into Jayden the second time.

*Yep. It's only a five-minute walk from the bus. I'll run over there now, then I can show you where we're parked. See you soon!*

I was in such a hurry to reach the front of the bus that I collided with Mike near the door.

"Whoa, girl. What are you all excited about?"

"Logan's here!" I grinned and slammed the button to release the front door. "I'm going to meet him. I'll be right back!"

Mike just chuckled as I hopped down the bus steps.

Evening air washed over my cheeks as I began to jog. Nighttime had fully set in, bringing with it the distant yips of coyotes. I ran through the grass, my excitement quickening my steps. It grew darker as I approached the trees, but my grin didn't fade as I kept my eyes peeled for Logan.

The park didn't have security lights, but thanks to the moonlight, I made out a parked car in the parking lot. *Probably a rental.*

"Logan?" I called.

"Over here."

I twirled in the direction of his voice, squinting since I could only make out random dark shapes. "Where are you?"

"Just over here."

I frowned. He sounded strange. I took a step closer. "Where?"

A rustling sound came from the forest, and a figure emerged. *Logan!*

Rushing forward, I said, "I'm so glad you're here!" I was about to throw my arms around him when warning flags abruptly waved in my mind.

I skidded to a stop. The outline of the man was slightly smaller than Logan's large build, but it did look familiar. "Jayden?"

Jayden lunged forward and grabbed my arm. I yelped as his fingers encircled my bicep, digging cruelly into my flesh.

"What the hell, Jayden?" I tried to pull my arm back, but his grip held firm. I yanked my arm again to no avail. "Where's Logan?"

"Logan's not here, but we are."

My heart slammed against my ribs as panic roared through me. My eyes widened as I recalled the text messages from my supposed boyfriend—and the new phone number.

I swallowed tightly.

Just because the person on the other end said he was Logan didn't mean he actually was. *But he called me babe and talked about his trip from California! Jayden couldn't have known that!*

Jayden tsk-tsked. "Little girls shouldn't leave their phones unlocked and sitting unattended on picnic tables. Especially when messages from their boyfriends pop up. Did you know that Logan just arrived at Bozeman's airport? Huh, *babe?* It was too easy to retrieve your number, delete his message, then pretend to be your boyfriend."

Jayden grinned. In the moonlight, his teeth appeared longer than they had before. They glistened with saliva and looked sharper. Deadly.

I shrank back, but his grip became steel. Sparks shot along my nerves before painful jolts slid down my arm as my light rushed out of its storage chest. Except that time, any sensation of Jayden being a potential mate vanished. *What the hell's happening?*

"Let me go, Jayden!" I tried to yank my arm back again.

But he merely leaned down, his eyes glowing red. "Too bad your SF boyfriend is still thirty minutes away. We should be long gone by then." He licked his lips and inhaled. "You smell so good, witch. Good enough to eat."

# Chapter 5

I screamed and tried to rip my arm free from Jayden's grip while kicking at his legs, but both proved useless.

I mumbled a telekinetic spell under my breath, but Jayden slapped a hand over my face, making it hard to breathe, let alone fight. "No spells, witch."

Still, I tried. I punched, kicked, and pushed against him as hard as I could while my mind reeled. *Jayden's attacking me? Why the hell is he attacking me?*

But my fighting did no good.

Jayden threw his head back and laughed, momentarily stopping my movements.

My blood turned cold. He wasn't the same person I'd met earlier. Any resemblance to the carefree, funny guy I'd met in the grocery store that morning had vanished.

"Who are you?" My voice was muffled against his hand.

Red light glowed in his eyes again, like embers coaxed to a flame. "Does it matter?" His voice grew deeper, more gravelly. He sounded almost *inhuman.*

A cold shudder ran through me.

I shook my head vigorously, but his palm wouldn't budge. Flailing, I tried again to break free. I needed to run. Get help. Have someone save me. Fight back. Disappear. Something. Anything!

*Holy shit, I'm losing it!* But this couldn't be happening. Not again. *How can I be attacked again within the span of a week?*

Growls came from my left. My mouth went dry. Two huge wolves emerged from the trees. *Niles and Zach!*

I fought harder, even though my knees threatened to give out as my stomach heaved. *They're rogues! They're fucking rogues! They have to be!*

I thrashed and fought, but Jayden's grip only strengthened. Bile rose in the back of my throat, and I yanked my arm back as hard as I could while biting down on his hand.

He yelped, and I managed to get out another half-cast spell before Jayden turned into a blur. His thick hand clamped over my mouth again, cutting off my magic, before he pinned me to him from behind. The feel of his chest rubbing against my back made sweat erupt across my entire body.

Niles and Zach advanced, long canines bared, their stalking steps as silent as bat wings in the night. One of them whined, the sound anxious.

"Shut up! I don't care who S wants us hunting! I want her," Jayden snarled.

*S?* I fought more, not understanding any of what Jayden was saying.

"I'll move her into the woods. Then we can all enjoy this tasty morsel. I bet her flesh is divine." Glee filled Jayden's voice as horror consumed me.

*Tasty morsel? Does that mean he's going to eat me? Or rape me?*

Sheer terror fueled my kicks, adrenaline rushing through me in waves, yet it did no good. Jayden's hand stopped my spells, and my flailing movements did little against his Herculean strength. He picked me up as if I were as light as a feather then jogged into the woods.

*How can this be happening? This can't be happening!*

The rough run jostled me in his arms. Niles and Zach followed us. Their eyes also glowed red as their tongues lolled out of their mouths. Excited whines erupted from their snouts, the earlier anxious-sounding ones gone.

Uncomfortable jolts from Jayden's touch traveled up my arms as the gravity of my situation took hold.

Logan wasn't there. I had no idea when he would be. I was on my own. Nobody was coming to save me.

*Jayden's going to kill me!*

Tears sprouted in my eyes, blurring my vision. It was possible that I would never see Logan again or never see Cecile and Mike again. I was only twenty-one years old, yet my life could be over before it really began.

A sob shook my chest, then another.

"Are you crying, sweetheart?" Jayden chuckled against my ear. The feel of his hot breath near my skin made me shiver.

*How could I have been so wrong about him?*

He stopped running when we entered a clearing. Clouds moved in front of the moon, casting everything into darkness. The onslaught of energy from Jayden hadn't abated. It felt like bugs crawled under my skin.

"Please. Don't do this!" I said against his hand.

He removed his calloused palm and turned me in his arms. His eyes were glowing so brightly that they reminded me of bloodred rubies. "If you try to cast a spell again, witch, I'll slash your throat."

He lifted his hand. From the tip of one fingernail, a claw emerged. It grew right before my eyes, turning into a sharp, razor-like blade two inches long.

I gulped. "You tricked me, made me think you were nice."

Jayden laughed again. "It was too easy."

Niles and Zach stopped just behind him, slinking against his sides. I could finally tell them apart now. Niles was the bigger, leaner one, whereas Zach was the smaller but thicker one.

Jayden set me on my feet. The ground swayed beneath me as my knees threatened to buckle.

"Please don't do this!" I cried desperately.

As Jayden towered above me, dark energy rolled off him. "Boys, I think she's scared." He laughed again.

Niles whined in excitement then opened his mouth, revealing razor-sharp teeth.

Jayden loosened his grip for a moment. I stiffened when the horrible effects of Jayden's touch stopped. But as soon as that clarity arrived, so did a flash of reason.

*Run, Daria! Run now!*

I tore free, shoving him hard before sprinting away.

"Bitch!" Jayden yelled. "Get her!"

A yelp of excitement came from behind me. Cold wind flew across my cheeks as my feet pounded the ground. I'd never been a fast runner, but the many hikes I did in my spare time had made my legs strong, and the adrenaline pumping through my veins made me faster.

I muttered a spell, the words coming out choked as I struggled to breathe. But the spell failed, my cadence incorrect as I gasped in air.

The forest grew closer as the edge of the clearing appeared. *Just get away! Forget about spells!* My hair whipped behind me. *Almost there!*

Something jumped on my back.

I flew forward and landed hard in the grass, knocking the wind out of me. Four paws pinned me to the earth. A growl came next before a mouth descended to my ear.

My diaphragm kicked back into action, and I sucked in a lungful of air. A bloodcurdling scream tore from my mouth. It was filled with panic and was loud enough to wake the dead.

I tried again to get the wolf off me, but he was too heavy.

A hand clamped over my face, cutting off any oxygen while pinning me harder to the earth. "Now, now, sweetheart. We can't be having that." Jayden flipped me over onto my back.

Niles and Zach closed in. They had me circled, and I was flat on the ground. Defenseless.

*No!*

"Well, boys. Let's not put this off any longer. Let's enjoy this delicious morsel once and for all."

Before my very eyes, Jayden began to shift. Hair sprouted on the backs of his hands as his mouth elongated into a snout, though the blood red of his eyes stayed the same. The air around him began to shimmer as his form changed from that of a man to a wolf.

His hand stayed on my mouth, rendering any spell casting impossible. The sensation of his skin changing from hand to paw, back and forth, caused bile to rise in my throat, making me want to gag.

Niles and Zach came closer, their mouths opening as each of them prepared to lunge forward, their haunches bent like tightly coiled springs.

They paused, ready, and it briefly registered that they were following Jayden's lead, waiting for him to shift.

I kept fighting, kept thrashing, but it did no good. Jayden held me, even while he shifted, as if I were a bug he played with on the sidewalk.

Still, I didn't stop. I fought and fought, despite my vision threatening to go dark from lack of oxygen.

I closed my eyes tightly, not wanting to see them bite me. Already, images of them tearing my flesh away, mouthful by mouthful, were filling my mind.

*This is it. I'm going to die.*

As Jayden shifted, increasing energy from him swirled into me. I'd never felt anything like it. It was evilness in its purest form, so very dark and black, as if the devil himself were before me.

My stomach heaved.

I flailed again, my vision dimming to a tunnel as

unconsciousness loomed. *I'm going to die. They're going to kill me.* Of that, I was certain.

Absolute terror filled my core, slicing along my limbs and consuming me from the inside out. *I'm going to die!*

Just as that gut-clenching, bone-deep realization hit home, something cracked deep within me, like a fissure in the earth.

My eyes flashed opened, but my vision still threatened to go dark.

Jayden's hand fully turned to a paw, the less effective appendage allowing me to breathe better. I sucked in a lungful of air. *What the hell?*

The fissure within me widened, like my insides were opening to a dark, hidden cave, then energy burst to the surface of my skin like a powerful earthquake.

I screamed, and my back arched off the ground, displacing Jayden's shifted paw, as swirling, immense power rose inside me like a burning inferno.

*What's happening?*

Dark powerful energy exploded along my limbs.

Niles clamped down on my leg, his teeth sinking into me. I screamed as pain ripped through my calf.

He bit deeper, and I screamed again as instinct simultaneously took over.

I lurched forward and grabbed ahold of Jayden's arm, which had become a front leg. It was still fleshy but covered with coarse hair. With my other hand, I reached for Niles's paw. I curled my fingers tightly around both as the power within me became stronger and stronger.

"What the hell?" Jayden said. He hadn't fully finished shifting, and his voice sounded guttural and thick, barely human.

Zach lunged at me, but I kicked him in the neck in a surprisingly fast move. He yelped and fell back.

My new power grew and grew, swirling within my core, and my grip on the rogues tightened.

Niles yelped, and Jayden fell to his knees. My fingers dug into them more.

Teeth bared, Zach advanced again, but then he paused. His massive head swung back and forth to look at his two friends, wariness showing in his bloodred eyes. Both of his friends screamed and convulsed in agony.

Zach shrank to the ground, his tail between his legs. In a flash of movement, he twirled around and ran. The last thing I saw was his bushy tail disappearing into the trees.

I kept my grip on Jayden and Niles and slowly came to my feet. They continued to writhe in pain as I instinctively called upon the new dark power.

I had no idea what was happening, and it felt like I wasn't in control of my body. Fear consumed me, but that emotion was there then gone, instinct claiming me.

*Push it out. Push your power into them with everything you have!*

The silent instructions came from deep within my mind, like an intrinsic, dormant consciousness had sprung to life.

I closed my eyes and did as the voice instructed. In a way, the darkness felt similar to my healing powers, when I burned all of the diseases away from sick clients until the light burst from my fingertips.

Except this new power wasn't light.

And I wasn't ridding myself of someone's disease.

Instead, I was harnessing the cold darkness inside me and pushing it into them.

The energy shot from my fingertips and exploded into Jayden and Niles. Blinding red light flew from my hands. Both of them screamed, the sound between that of an animal and a human.

I felt it when they died.

I felt the energy crush their bones, mince their muscle fibers, and squeeze their hearts into pulverized flesh. Both of them fell slack in my hands before falling into heaps on the ground as the pulsing red light subsided from my hands.

Panting, I stared at the carnage in front of me—the death, the decay, the smell. *Oh my god, the smell!*

My knees gave out, and I fell to the ground.

*What just happened?* My breathing increased, my chest feeling as though it would explode. Inside me, the cold darkness subsided, but it stayed low in my belly, not returning to whatever cavern it had emerged from.

*What's happening?*

I held my hands up in the moonlight, staring at them as if they were foreign objects I couldn't identify, but all that stared back were small hands, each with five fingers.

Yet they were hands that didn't feel like mine.

I had no idea what the swirling darkness inside me was, but something had just unleashed—something beyond my control.

I stared again at the two dead bodies on the ground, one partially shifted. *Oh god! Oh god! Oh god!*

Terror coiled around my belly like a deadly python,

my jaw dropping as the implications of what had just happened set in. I'd just killed two people. Me. A healer, a giver of life, had just *killed*.

"What did I just do?" I whispered and curled up in a ball on the ground between the dead werewolves.

A shout sounded in the distance. Someone was calling my name. *Logan*.

My hands shook so badly that I dug my fingers into my thighs to stop their trembling.

"Daria!" His frantic cry came again.

"Over here!" Even though the words flowed from my lips, the voice didn't sound like mine. It sounded hoarse, panicked, like the words had come from a person I no longer knew.

A person who killed.

Logan, Cecile, and Mike burst from the forest into the clearing. They were on the other side, at least a hundred yards away, yet Logan's eyes glowed. Even from the distance, I could see them. They were like two dim headlights. When he spotted me, he turned into a blur, leaving Cecile and Mike behind.

One minute, he was across the clearing, and the next minute, he was hauling me against him so hard that I thought he would crush me.

"Daria! Oh shit, Daria!" He cradled my face in his hands, tilting my chin upward. Bright eyes, stormy with panic, gazed down at me.

The dark power rushed up the second he touched me. Panic seized me, and I scrambled to get out of his arms as he said in a rush, "Thank God you're okay. Mike said I'd contacted you, but I didn't. I thought the worst. I thought—"

"Logan, you need to let me go! I could—"

But it was like he didn't hear me. His entire body stiffened, his nostrils flaring. His head whipped to face the wolves. In a lightning-fast move, he released me and stood over the dead werewolves, or what was left of them.

I breathed a sigh of relief. As soon as his touch disappeared, the dark power calmed. I hadn't hurt Logan. I *hadn't* hurt him.

But as soon as that relief came so did the ramifications of what could have happened if he *hadn't* let go. Oh *my god . . . I could have hurt him. I could have killed him!*

But Logan remained oblivious to all that was spiraling inside me like a cyclone.

"Rogues," he said, his attention on the dead werewolves as his hands tightened into fists.

"Yes," was all I could manage. *Rogues that I killed with my bare hands.*

Blood had poured from Jayden and Niles, red rivers trailing down their ears, nostrils, mouths, and the corners of their eyes. And their bodies looked like a giant had taken them within his fists and crushed every bone inside them. They resembled rubbery, gelatinous masses, limp on the ground.

Logan scanned the clearing, taking in the scene. The moonlight played across his ruggedly handsome features. With each second that passed, his breath came faster as his jaw locked more.

"What happened?" he finally asked. His words sounded calm, in control, despite the chaos that littered the clearing.

Labored breathing caught my attention. Cecile and Mike stumbled to our sides, having finally caught up with Logan.

"Oh my goodness!" Cecile exclaimed when she saw the dead werewolves.

Mike pulled his hat off, his jaw dropping.

When Cecile looked back at me, her gaze widened. "Daria, you're bleeding!"

Blood flowed from the werewolf bite around my calf. Funnily enough, I hadn't felt it. Adrenaline still pounded through my veins.

"Dammit!" Logan ripped his shirt off, and in a blurred move, was back at my side, pressing it to my leg. "They bit you?" Barely controlled rage filled his tone.

I pulled away from him and held the shirt tightly to my wound, trembling. *Yes, they bit me, then I killed them. I'm a killer. I'm supposed to be a healer, but now I'm a killer.*

The brightness around Logan's irises grew.

I began to shake in earnest then. Violent shudders wracked my body as the cold dark power roiled in my belly. Whatever had been unleashed inside me during the attack hadn't gone away. If anything, it had grown. I felt its power, its strength, and I had no idea what it was.

Logan inched closer but seemed to sense my anxiety and didn't touch me. "Daria, you're safe now. Nobody's going to hurt you." He softened his tone. "Can you tell me what happened?"

I took a deep quivering breath. My hands still shook. My stomach still heaved. Logan's ripped shirt fluttered like a leaf in my hands. "I don't know. I killed them.

Somehow, with this new power inside me." I shook more, my entire body vibrating. "I'm a murderer. Oh my god, I'm a murderer!"

"Shh." Cecile came to my side.

Logan crouched down, too, while Cecile tried to soothe me without touching me and igniting my light, yet despite their concern, I'd never felt more alone.

"What new power?" Logan asked.

At the same time, Cecile asked, "What are rogues?"

Logan's attention stayed on me when he answered Cecile. He seemed to be assessing the rest of my body for injuries. "Rogues are werewolves that have left the community to set out on their own. We're pack creatures by nature, and we're not meant to live alone. When we do, we change. All rogues are murderous." His nostrils flared again. "But these have a smell to them I can't identify. They don't smell like normal rogue werewolves. They carry an undercurrent of decay and . . ." He leaned down and sniffed more. "Sulfur."

Cecile and Mike shared concerned looks, and the clenching in Logan's jaw continued.

My gaze darted to Jayden and Niles, but I quickly looked away as nausea threatened to empty my stomach.

"Let's get her out of here." Cecile pushed to stand. "We need to get her to a doctor."

"I can treat the wound, but we should get her back to the bus. I'll carry her." Logan reached for me tentatively, treating me like a scared animal that might bolt at any moment. That barely controlled rage still filled his eyes, but his tone stayed soothing. "Dar, I'm going to pick you up. All right? It's just me. Nobody's going to hurt you anymore. You're safe now."

I scurried away so fast that burning pain shot up my calf. "No, Logan! You can't touch me!" The dark power rolled within me, all along my limbs. It wasn't locked away, not like my light. Instead, the darkness rushed upward the more my fear grew, just as violently as before.

Logan stopped advancing, but he, Cecile, and Mike shared more concerned looks, obviously having no understanding of what had happened to me. Hell, even I didn't know, but at the moment, the darkness threatened to rise up inside me again.

Cecile's tone turned soothing. "Honey, we need to go back to the bus and—" She looked at Logan. "Then what do we do?"

Logan whipped his cell phone out. "I'll handle this. I need to call this in anyway, and we'll need a cleanup crew for them." His jaw clenched tightly when he eyed the rogues.

After he finished his call, which consisted of a few terse sentences, Logan slipped his phone back into his pocket then undid his belt. "Daria?" His tone became gentle again, that deep, soothing rumble. "I need to cinch this around your leg to stop the bleeding." In the moonlight, his chiseled chest rose and fell heavily with every breath he took. Despite his calm demeanor, I could tell that inside, he was anything but calm.

"I'll do it." I grabbed the belt from him, careful to not touch him, before tightening it around my calf and hissing when it stung. The puncture wounds went deep, but I could probably still walk.

The light around Logan's irises grew, but he didn't

argue when I awkwardly rose from the ground and began hobbling. The three of them followed.

"Which way?" I asked when I realized I had no idea how to get back to the bus.

Logan stepped forward, his tone soft. "This way. Just follow me, babe."

I fell into step beside him as Cecile and Mike brought up the rear. The two of them spoke quietly, falling back and putting distance between us, but I still overheard their conversation.

"Thank goodness we set out looking for her as soon as Logan showed up. If we hadn't—"

"It's okay, Cece. We found her in time, and she's safe. Although from the looks of it back there, she didn't need our help."

"But was that Jayden? It looked like Jayden, I mean kind of. His face was so distorted. And does that mean he attacked her?"

I swallowed sharply, hurried forward, and did my best to tune them out. Already, horrifying images of the three rogues attacking me threatened to overwhelm me, and the power in my belly grew again at a frightening pace.

*No! Stay down! Please stay down!*

I was thankful that Logan didn't press me for any more details or say anything on the walk back, but he did continually look at me, worry etched so deeply in his face it was as if an artist had sculpted his features in fear. All the while, the new dark power swirled around inside me like angry clouds threatening to unleash a storm.

But as much as the power scared me, I also knew that if it *hadn't* sprung forth from wherever it resided, at that very moment, I would be dead.

As scary as it was, it had saved me.

# Chapter 6

Despite the air being cool, Logan didn't seem to mind being shirtless. His scent fluttered to me as I limped back to the bus.

Normally, his toned muscles and alluring sandalwood fragrance would have had me drifting closer to him, but at the moment, all I felt was sick.

Touching him could mean his death.

When my home finally came into view, Logan's gaze slid over my leg. "We'll need to clean that," he said in that gentle voice again. "Werewolf bites are nasty, but since you're a supernatural, you'll probably be fine. Still . . . we should clean it."

"Will I turn into a werewolf now since I've been bitten?"

"No. Only men can be werewolves. You'll be fine."

"But if I were a man, would I turn into a werewolf? That's what all the movies say, that if a werewolf bites you, you become one."

"Yes, a bite from a mature werewolf can turn someone, but it's not that easy. There's a process, and a quick bite to your leg won't do it."

I wanted to ask more, anything to distract myself from what had happened, but when we reached the bus, Logan hopped up the stairs. He turned, offering me his hand.

"I'll manage." I grabbed the railing. "And Logan, I can't explain what happened to me, but you can't touch me. I'm serious. You can't. This new power inside me, it could kill you."

I was vaguely aware that I sounded hysterical.

A deep groove settled between Logan's eyes, but his tone remained calm. "Okay, I won't touch you. I promise. Let me get the couch ready for you. Can you get up the stairs?"

"Yes." I hobbled up the steps awkwardly as he made room for me on the sofa.

The sound of Mike and Cecile approaching the bus reached my ears. They'd fallen far behind us, obviously sensing that close contact with anyone would freak me out, but hearing their voices made me bustle forward.

When I plopped down on the couch unceremoniously, Logan crouched at my side.

I took in his exquisite features. More than anything, I wanted to lay my palm across his cheek and touch my lips to his. A deep ache over the fact that he waited so close yet felt so far away grew in my belly.

I still hadn't properly touched him, and everything about him looked so familiar: his broad shoulders, square jaw, chocolate-brown eyes, and dark hair. His scent kept drifting my way, too, that sandalwood scent I loved so much.

Yet even though I'd spent the past week dreaming of seeing him again, it had never been under such circumstances, and I'd certainly never been terrified of touching him.

A shrill laugh bubbled up my throat. Only an hour ago, I'd been eagerly awaiting his return.

But now . . .

I trembled again.

The groove between his eyes deepened. "The SF cleanup crew is on its way, and even though I'm guessing you don't want to talk about what happened back there with strangers, there are going to be a lot of questions. This incident will likely open an investigation. Whatever happened and the way you killed them . . ." He shook his head. "I've never seen anything like it."

Nervous energy filled my body. The dark power responded, as if knowing I was thinking about it. It swirled and rolled in my belly like an unborn child. I hastily rearranged myself on the couch, hissing when I jarred my leg.

Logan's frown grew just as Cecile and Mike climbed aboard the bus.

"Oh good! You're sitting down!" Cecile bustled ahead of Mike to my side.

"Can one of you get the first aid kit?" Logan asked.

"I'll grab it." Mike brushed past us, heading to the bathroom at the back of the bus. The old door in the back squeaked open as Mike dug around in the cabinet for the kit.

Cecile busied herself, too, hurrying to the kitchen while mumbling something about getting warm water to wash my wound.

Logan stayed crouched at my side, his jaw locked while that heavy frown marred his chiseled features.

I sighed. "Go ahead. I know you want to ask questions. It's okay, really."

He opened his mouth but hesitated before asking, "Did you really kill them by yourself?"

"Yes." A pit formed in my stomach. I'd killed two people. Granted, they were trying to kill *me*, but I'd never killed anyone before. *I'm a killer now. I'm a killer.* My breath hitched.

"Daria? Stay with me. They were rogues. *Two* rogues. I'm still trying to wrap my head around it."

"There weren't two. There were three."

"*What?*" Logan jumped up.

The bustling at the back of the bus stopped. Mike stood near Cecile in the kitchen, the first aid kit in his hands forgotten, while Cecile held a pot of steaming liquid. Both wore startled expressions.

"Where's the third one?" Logan asked, already assessing the dark park outside the windows.

"Zach ran off."

"Zach? You knew him?"

"I knew all of them. It was Jayden and his two friends."

Logan kneeled back at my side, tension oozing from his shoulders like malevolent energy. His gaze continually darted to the windows while he intermittently sniffed the air. "Are you telling me the guy at the grocery store who hit on you is the rogue who attacked you?"

I tightly laced my hands together so he wouldn't see me shaking. All I managed was a nod.

"But I thought he was a . . . potential mate." Those last two words seemed to pain him.

"So did I." I unlaced my fingers and folded my shaking arms around myself, still trying to understand something that wasn't understandable. "I didn't know they were rogues. I . . . just . . ." My lip trembled. "Jayden seemed so normal, nice even, and he told me they were part of the community and that they lived together. That's not something rogues normally do, right? Isn't that what you told me? That they live alone? Right?" I was briefly aware that I was sounding hysterical again.

"That's right."

I shook my head. "They tricked me, then Jayden texted me tonight, pretending to be you. I fell for it. It's the only reason I left the bus. I shouldn't have believed that text. I should have called to make sure it was you. I should have—"

"Shh." Logan moved closer, his bare chest brushing against my leg for the merest moment.

My light stayed calm in the chest I stored it in, but the dark power rushed upward. I hastily inched back just as something between a sob and a laugh erupted from me. "I'm just like my mom! Our bodies think monsters can be mates!"

A golden glow lit Logan's eyes. His jaw locked as he retrieved the first aid kit and water from Cecile and Mike. Both Mike and Cecile stood speechless.

Almost absentmindedly, Logan began washing my wound, being careful not to make direct contact with my skin.

Logan moved the rag up and down my leg gently. Warm water trickled down my calf, stinging my wound.

"So Jayden was a rogue, yet you handled him by yourself, and you also killed the second one." He shook his head. "That's unheard of. Rogues are notoriously strong. Only the strongest survive outside of the community. They usually fight when they come into contact with another rogue. Those battles only have one victor, yet you killed them both and only have one bite to show for it." His movements paused, his frown deepening.

"Do all rogues have red eyes? Is that another way to identify them?"

"Red eyes? What are you talking about?"

"They all had glowing red eyes, not gold like yours."

"*Red* eyes? Are you sure?"

"Very sure."

"I've never heard of any werewolf having red eyes." Logan dropped the rag in the water before pulling out antiseptic. I bit back a yelp when he poured it generously over my wound. It bubbled on contact.

He winced. "Sorry, but I need to clean this."

Mike and Cecile finally sat on the opposite couch, but that fearful look in their eyes remained. Neither of them commented or interrupted Logan, though, as if knowing they were completely out of their element regarding all of this.

Logan opened the first aid kit and pulled out clean gauze. He gently wrapped it around my leg. "Babe, can you tell me what happened? All of it? From the beginning? I imagine it's hard to talk about, but we'll need as much information as you can give us to get to the bottom of this."

I shivered, remembering that strange dormant power that had exploded within me when the thick evil from Jayden had swirled around him. It was as though I'd opened Pandora's box. I licked my dry lips. "I don't know exactly, but something . . . happened to me when they were going to eat me—"

"Eat you?" Cecile shrieked.

Logan growled, the sound deep in his throat. "It's what rogues do. It's why I told Daria to run if she ever encountered any."

"And instead I invited them to dinner," I said shrilly.

"Well, technically, they invited themselves." Mike shrugged.

I laughed, thankful for the joke.

"You had dinner with them?" Logan shook himself. "Not important right now. So what happened . . . in the woods?" he prodded gently.

I leaned back, using the soft feel of the gauze wrapping around my leg as a distraction from the terror that wanted to consume me. I explained the strange power that had risen inside me after Jayden had carried me into the woods, how I'd kicked off Zach, and he'd run away in fear, and how I'd harnessed the new power.

"That power killed them. And when it burst from my fingertips, the color was red, not gold like my healing light, but red like the color of their eyes."

"Red again." Logan's frown grew.

Cecile's eyebrows knit together. "So what does that mean? Daria's mother and grandmother never spoke of anything like that happening to them."

I shivered again and took a deep breath. "Maybe there's something wrong with me."

A dark look flashed across Logan's face. "There's nothing wrong with you. Whatever that new power is, it kept you alive."

∞ ∞ ∞

As Logan prowled around inside the bus, keeping an eye out for Zach through the windows, I mulled over everything that had happened.

In a way, I was glad Logan had prodded me to tell him. Already, details of the evening were fading, but talking about it helped keep it clearer in my mind.

"Here, honey. I've got some ibuprofen for you." Cecile handed me two tablets before picking up the discarded first aid supplies.

I swallowed them hastily just as a howl penetrated the night. Her eyes widened, darting to the windows.

"Coyotes," Logan said, glancing at his watch as he stalked past us for the third time. His heavy footsteps made the bus shake. "Not wolves, and not a werewolf."

Mike, still sitting on the opposite couch, took his hat off and smoothed his mustache. "You can tell the difference?"

Logan nodded. "To a werewolf, the howl of another werewolf carries a unique cadence. Humans can't detect it, but we can. It's how we identify each other in the wild and how we know where our pack is."

"So if Zach is around here, and he howled, you'd know it was him?" I asked.

"I'd know it was a werewolf howling, but since I don't know if I've ever met Zach, I can't tell you for sure if I'd recognize his *ululate*."

Cecile cocked her head. "Ululate?"

"It's what we call a werewolf's unique howl. Jake has a talent for memorizing and storing all ululates he's encountered, and while I do okay with it, my memory isn't as good as his. If Jake were here, he could tell you if he'd ever encountered Zach in his lifetime after hearing his howl."

Cecile scrunched the garbage in her hands. "I had no idea."

"I imagine most humans have no idea." Mike winked, getting another smile out of me.

Cecile swatted the trash at him before putting it in the garbage.

"So now what?" she asked while eyeing the park through the window. With the lights on inside the bus, we couldn't see much outside, mostly just our reflections, and I would have bet money that made Cecile nervous.

"Now we wait for the SF cleanup crew." Logan checked his watch again. "They should be here any minute, which means this place will be swarming with Supernatural Forces members in no time. It should be safe to spend the night here despite what happened."

Cecile let out a breath, her shoulders relaxing. "Thank the stars."

Logan swiveled his chocolate-colored eyes my way. "My boss is coming with them. He'll want to talk to you about what happened tonight. You'll have to tell him everything from the beginning."

Uneasily, I swallowed. "Okay. I can do that, but is that normal? For him to come to a scene when something like this happens?"

That deep groove appeared between Logan's eyes again. "No. I can't remember the last time he left our headquarters to partake in a cleanup."

# Chapter 7

Knowing I was going to have to talk to Logan's boss made anxiety swirl inside me like a buzzing hornet's nest that had fallen from the rafters.

Seeming to sense my unease, Logan stopped pacing and sat at my side. Just having him close helped, but still…

*His boss!*

When a sea of people suddenly appeared out of thin air in the clearing, I yelped.

"That's the SF. They used portal keys." Logan raised his palm, as if he intended to place it comfortingly over mine. At the last moment, he pulled his hand back, his jaw tightening. "They probably would have been here sooner, but the number of portal keys they had to acquire was higher than normal."

"So you don't normally travel that way?"

He shook his head. "Portal keys are infused with strong magic. They're very precious. We use them sparingly, but considering the gravity of this situation, they obviously made an exception." He rose from the couch. "Do you want to join me?"

I pushed up and swung my leg over the side of the sofa. The throbbing had lessened, thanks to the dose of ibuprofen Cecile had given me, but it still hurt.

I hobbled after Logan down the stairs while Cecile and Mike glued themselves to the windows.

"It's a good thing this park is quiet," I said when Logan released the bus door. It hissed open, and cool air washed over my cheeks. "Otherwise, the locals would probably be asking why there are so many people around here." *People wearing dark suits and helmets and appearing from thin air.*

"The locals can't see what's happening right now." Logan jogged down the steps and waited for me at the bottom. He held out his hand for me, but I shook my head. "Sorry, habit."

I smiled sadly, my gaze traveling up his frame. He looked incredibly sexy with the moonlight dipping his chiseled features into shadows. More than anything, I wanted to press myself flush against him and get lost in his kiss, anything to forget what had happened.

As if reading my thoughts, his eyes began to glow. A knowing look crossed his face before he inhaled. No doubt my interest was giving off that scent he loved so much.

Shaking my head, I forced myself to step down the

stairs carefully. At the bottom, Logan again shifted closer to me. I doubted he even knew he was doing it.

"Did you really say the locals can't see any of this?" I asked.

He nodded. "If someone walked by, all they would see is your bus with the lights off and a quiet park empty of people."

"How is that possible?"

"Holly is already taking care of our coverage. She's a witch employed by the SF and specializes in cloaking spells."

I stepped onto the park's lawn behind Logan, once again realizing how much I had to learn. "I'm guessing cloaking spells hide things? I've never learned any cloaking spells. To be honest, I didn't even know some witches could do that." That was way beyond my simple spells and incantations. "But how do you know she's already doing it?"

He pointed upward. "That's how."

I gasped when I saw a thin, shimmery dome surrounding the bus and the park. "You can *see* her cloaking spell?"

"*We* can. Humans can't."

Through the magical cloaking spell, moonlight poured over the Supernatural Forces squad. The strong moonlight along with the lights that shone from the SF's headlamps made it easy to see everything.

At least two dozen men and women patrolled the park. The SF members were of various shapes and sizes, making me guess the Supernatural Forces employed more than just werewolves and a witch who specialized in cloaking spells.

Some members of the SF team carried high tech equipment, others sniffed the air while following a trail I couldn't see, and a few huddled together, discussing who knew what.

"Logan," a woman purred before sidling up to my boyfriend and draping her hands on his shoulders. "I've missed you. I haven't had the pleasure of working with you in a while."

I froze midstep, watching the woman's fingers trail down his bicep. She touched him so easily, as if she knew him well. And unlike me, touching others obviously didn't trigger her magic.

Jealousy coursed through me at lightning speed, but I took comfort in one thing—Logan immediately stepped away from her, breaking any contact they shared.

"Holly." He nodded curtly.

She gave a rich, throaty laugh. "Logan, so formal!" She continued to smile, but that smile turned to plastic when she looked at me.

I stood up straighter. Holly towered above me by at least six inches, and her willowy figure provoked images of runway lingerie models.

Skintight leather pants covered her shapely legs, three-inch heels graced her feet, and a form-fitting red top accentuated her every curve. Everything about her was designed to draw attention, including the thick bright-red hair draping down her back.

I forced a smile. "Hi. I'm Daria Gresham."

She put a hand on her hip, her lips curving upward, reminding me of a cat waiting to pounce. "Well, hello,

Daria Gresham. I hear you've finally become aware of the community." She tossed her long dyed-red hair over her shoulder. "Mommy isn't around to keep you away from us anymore, huh?"

Any openness I had felt toward giving Holly a fair chance vanished. As if responding, the dark power swirled up inside me. Just the feel of its sheer power made my eyes widen.

I hastily took a step back as I tried to stuff it into the chest where I stored my healing light, but it wouldn't budge.

Holly laughed again, apparently interpreting my retreat as a sign of intimidation versus what it actually was—fear that I would kill her, even though at the moment, that seemed rather appealing.

Logan growled and stepped closer to me. "Holly, Daria's my girlfriend. Try to show some respect. Her mother died last year."

Holly brought a hand to her throat. "Oh, she did? I'm sorry. I didn't know."

*Yeah, right.*

Holly's eyes narrowed. "And did you say girlfriend?" She guffawed. "You can't be serious, Logan. What about Crystal?"

*Crystal again?* I frowned. I knew of Crystal. She'd texted Logan while he'd worked as my bodyguard, but he'd told me that she wasn't his girlfriend but simply a girl from back home.

Logan's hands clenched into fists. "Watch yourself, Holly."

She laughed again, that deep, throaty sound that made

a few heads turn. "Why? Are you afraid little Daria will learn the truth?"

She winked my way before sauntering off, waving her hand with graceful strokes as her hips swayed provocatively.

The air shimmered around her fingers, iridescent colors glimmering in her wake. The hazy dome above us brightened behind her, as if strengthened by whatever magic she wove.

If my mind hadn't been reeling from what she'd just said, I would have stepped forward to see if I could feel her magical barrier or to watch what happened when I stepped through it. As it was, I turned toward Logan with my hands on my hips.

"What did she mean by that?" I hated that I sounded jealous, but that was exactly how my sharp tone came across.

Logan opened his mouth, his gaze shifting, but another newcomer interrupted.

"Logan? Is that Daria with you?"

A man marched to Logan's side. From his size, I guessed werewolf blood flowed in his veins. He stood around Logan's height and had arms so thick that they reminded me of tree trunks. Given the rigid way the man carried himself, I guessed he was in the SF. But he appeared much older than Logan. Gray hair lined his head, and deep wrinkles cut grooves into the corners of his eyes.

Logan's shoulders drew back. "Yes, sir. This is Daria Gresham. Daria, this is my boss, Wes McCloy."

Wes nodded curtly. "Nice to finally meet you, Daria,

although I can't say I'm happy about the circumstances. Logan tells me you had an encounter with several rogues." A buzz emitted from his pocket. He pulled out a high-tech-looking tablet and typed in a few things before putting it away. "Their cleanup is proving to be more difficult than we anticipated. We've tried to pick them up, but they disintegrate into a jellylike substance. I have to say, that's a first."

The state that I'd left Jayden and Niles in flew through my mind. My mouth went dry.

"Which brings me to one of many questions," he continued. "How did they get in that state?"

When I opened my mouth to reply, no words came out. Even though Logan had warned me there would be questions, my heart still beat erratically.

A rumbling growl filled Logan's chest. He stepped closer to me. "Do you want to go in the bus and sit down? Will it be easier if you're in your home while talking about it?"

Wes waved toward the bus. "That's a good idea." His tone grew softer, but it wasn't as soothing as Logan's. I had a sneaking suspicion my boyfriend had more experience in the field. I probably wasn't the first trauma victim he'd dealt with.

"We'll take it slow," Logan continued when I just stood there. "And remember, you're safe now. No one's going to hurt you."

The way his tone dropped and the deep, protective growl that followed it soothed my frayed nerves. Still, I shivered. "Yeah, that's fine. Let's go on the bus, and I'll answer your questions."

In the distance, Holly watched us. So did a few other SF members. I didn't know if they could hear us, but it felt like everyone was trying to listen in.

My legs felt like wooden sticks when we climbed back aboard the bus.

"Has your leg been treated?" Wes asked when I limped up the stairs. "Logan says one of them bit you."

"Logan cleaned it with antiseptic then wrapped it with gauze."

Wes nodded curtly. "Good. Make sure it stays clean. Our kind leaves a nasty bite."

Once the three of us entered the living space, Cecile and Mike jumped up from where they'd been crouched with their noses pressed to the windows like two kids peering into a haunted house.

"Would you like to have a seat?" I waved at the couches after the bus door hissed closed behind us.

Wes eyed the kitchen table. "How about there?"

Cecile straightened her hair, and Mike took his Yankees cap off.

"This is Wes," I said to them. "Logan's boss."

"Ah, how lovely." A smile plastered on Cecile's face. "I'll make some tea for everyone."

She hurried to the kitchen while Logan, his boss, and I settled around the table—Wes across from Logan and me. I made sure to keep a few inches of distance between Logan's thigh and mine. Mike hung back and returned his attention to the activity outside.

Within minutes, the teakettle whistled.

"There we are." Cecile placed mugs in front of everyone and smoothed her hair again. "I suppose I'll join

Mike." She hurried back to the front of the bus.

They would still be able to hear us if they wanted to, but since they sat in the very front, I knew they were trying to give us privacy.

Logan shifted in his seat, making his arm brush mine. He stiffened, as if aware of what he'd done.

The contact caused goose bumps to erupt along my skin, but more than that responded. The dark power roiled in my belly. I inched away more and blew on my mug of hot tea while I tried to wrangle the dark power into the storage chest with my light.

As before, it wouldn't submit.

"Do you mind if I ask you a few questions now?" Wes asked.

"That's fine. Go ahead." I gave up trying to wrestle the dark power and instead made sure I sat far enough away from Logan that I couldn't hurt him. When I tentatively sipped my tea, the hot brew scalded my tongue.

Wes pulled the tablet from his pocket again. I could feel Logan watching me, following my every move. My hand shook more when I set my tea down, earning me a worried frown from my boyfriend.

"I'd like to start by hearing your detailed account of what happened here tonight. Can you start at the beginning? I'd like to hear everything." Wes's fingers hovered over his tablet, as if he were going to record what I said.

"Well . . ." I shoved my hands under the table to hide that I was twisting them. "To start at the beginning, I'd have to go back to this morning, when I first met

Jayden."

Wes began typing on his tablet. "Go on."

I told him *everything*—about meeting Jayden at the supermarket, how he'd followed me to the park, and how he'd come to dinner with his friends. But when I got to the part of him tricking me and them trapping me in the woods, my voice caught.

"Once I got there, I quickly realized my mistake, but I wasn't strong enough to escape Jayden. He clamped a hand over my mouth and dragged me into the woods. Niles and Zach were there, too, except they'd both shifted into wolves. All three of them had glowing red eyes." I shuddered. "That really creeped me out."

Wes stopped typing. "Glowing red eyes?"

"Yeah, their eyes glowed red, not golden like Logan's."

Logan and his boss shared perplexed looks. Wes leaned forward more. "Describe their eyes to me."

I trembled as the memory of their ruby-red eyes and saliva-covered teeth swirled in my mind. "Their eyes looked like brightly burning coals. Deep red and filled with hate."

"Red eyes . . ." Wes typed more on his tablet, a heavy frown settling on his face. "That's the first I've heard of that in rogues, and from what you've described, they were also rogues working together. That's also unheard of." His frown deepened. "Then what happened?"

"He said something about a man named S." That tiny detail suddenly came to me. I'd almost forgotten about it. I described how Jayden had made a comment about me not being who they were supposed to be hunting. "I have no idea what he meant by that, but then I tried to run, and they pounced on me. Jayden started to shift as Niles lunged forward and bit me."

The further I delved into the story, the tenser Logan grew. His muscles strained, veins popping out of his forearms and neck. He looked like a volcano ready to blow.

"Logan?" Wes interrupted. "Do you need a minute?" He asked the question calmly, as if Logan's reaction were normal.

"No," Logan replied in a clipped tone. "I want to know what she went through."

More than anything, I wanted to place my hand on his, to reassure him that I was fine, but the dark power swirling in my belly had grown the more I talked about the rogues.

Even though I wasn't touching either Logan or Wes, anxiety still made me inch back more. Once again, I felt completely out of control of whatever had been born inside me.

I swallowed tightly then resumed talking. "And that's when I knew I was going to die. I couldn't run, they were too strong for me to fight, and it was three against one, but when I grabbed onto Jayden and Niles, I felt an evilness in them that I'd never felt before."

My mouth went dry despite the tea. "And in that moment, something cracked open inside me, and this rush of dark, cold power shot up, kind of like my healing light but different. It was stronger and sharper. Then a voice in my mind told me what to do—I still can't explain that—so I kicked Zach away and clamped my hands onto

Jayden and Niles." Sweat beaded on my forehead as my heart began to pound. Just remembering the details made me nauseous.

Logan shifted, coming closer to me, but when I flinched, he stopped. In a low, deep voice, he said soothingly, "It's okay, Dar. They're gone. They can't hurt you anymore."

Hearing his deep voice helped calm my racing heart. Licking my dry lips, I continued. "So I did what the voice said. I gathered my new dark power, and I shot it into them, then . . . they died, and what's left of them is in that clearing."

# Chapter 8

Wes leaned back with a stunned expression. "I've never heard of anything like that."

I squeezed my hands together. "That's what Logan said."

Wes shook his head, disbelief written all over his features. "You single-handedly killed *two* rogues and fought off a third. Do you know how hard that is? Three rogues would have killed anyone else."

At the reminder that I'd almost died, Logan balled his hands tightly into fists, as if they were hard boulders that desperately wanted to punch something.

I tried to give him a reassuring look.

"Yet you killed them with only your touch," Wes replied.

I grimaced. The dark power still swirled inside me. Similar to my light, it felt potent, but in a different way. Whereas my light was golden and airy, the dark felt cold and powerful.

Not wanting to dwell on it any further, I asked, "Has there been any sign of Zach?"

Wes shook his head. "He's probably on the run. Hopefully, we'll catch him." He tapped his chin, and a moment of silence passed before he said, "I have to admit, I'm curious if other witches can be trained to do what you did."

"Trained?" I cocked my head.

He leaned forward, a keen interest in his eyes. "Yes. You're a witch, correct? You can heal and do telekinetic spells?"

"Yes, but the spells and incantations I know are pretty simple. My family has always concentrated on our healing magic, not our telekinetic magic."

"It's common for witches to excel in certain areas of practice, yet you were still able to fight off rogues . . . as a *witch*. It's worth pursuing, to see if other witches can be trained to kill rogues too."

He said it so casually, as if being a killer was no big deal. But it *was* a big deal to me. My purpose was to give life, not to take it away.

Wes drained the rest of his tea and rose. "I think that's all of the questions I have for now. I'm going to join the team at the clearing. Logan, I think it's best if you stay with Daria until we have a better understanding of what happened here tonight."

Logan dipped his head. "Yes, sir."

"And, Daria, I'd like you to come to headquarters if you're able. If you can instruct other witches, the SF's ability to fight future rogues would increase."

"But I don't even know what I did."

"You may not now, but perhaps in time you will."

I wrung my hands. "I have to finish my healing tour before I could even think about doing that."

"I understand, but I would still like you to consider it." Wes shoved his tablet back into his pocket. "As for what happened here tonight, I'll be in touch if I need any further information."

∞　∞　∞

By the next morning, the shock of what had happened the previous night hadn't disappeared, but it had lessened. The dark power still flowed inside me, but I had a show in a few hours which meant I needed to focus.

And while nerves fluttered in my belly at the thought of performing, I took comfort in one thing: my healing power didn't require me to touch anyone. My hands always floated above a person during a healing session, and as long as the dark power stayed at bay if I *didn't* touch anyone, my clients would still be safe.

Logan glanced at me from where he stood by the small stove in the bus's kitchen. Given his frequent frowns and furrowed brow, I knew he was worried about me. Since Cecile and Mike had already finished their usual oatmeal and coffee, I sat alone at the small table near the kitchen while Logan cooked.

As usual, Logan wore jeans and a navy-blue T-shirt.

His strong shoulders stretched the thin fabric—something I was certain I would *never* grow tired of seeing.

More than a few times, I'd become distracted by the broadness of his shoulders and the strength of his hand while he gripped the spatula. Who knew cooking breakfast could be so sexy. Despite all that had happened, my lady bits still responded to him, but each time it happened, a heavy dose of frustration followed.

Who knew when—*if*—I would be able to touch him again.

*Ugh.*

Scents of scrambled eggs wafted through the air when he finished preparing our meal. He slid the plates filled with steaming eggs and toast onto the table, his finger brushing mine in the process. I stilled, but he pulled back quickly and retreated to the counter to grab napkins. Our shared contact had been so brief that my powers hadn't flared.

It was as if Logan had known that. Or, he was testing the new dark power and seeing what he could get away with.

*If only his hands could slide around my waist and pull me close. Like he had done before leaving for California—*

"We'll be there in less than an hour!" Mike called over his shoulder from the front of the bus.

Mike's abrupt statement snapped me from my wishful daydream. I forced a smile when Logan slid into the seat across from me, his eyebrow quirked in curiosity. I could only imagine the facial expression I wore.

I picked up my fork and tried to concentrate on my

upcoming show. Country music spilled from the speakers, and Mike whistled along, his hands on the large steering wheel. Western Montana loomed all around us as we sped down a highway. Jagged rocky peaks and lush valleys filled the windows.

The bus rumbled beneath my toes when Logan said, "I hope you're hungry." His deep voice vibrated through me, eliciting goose bumps on my arms.

I bit into a piece of toast and swallowed before saying, "Thank you for making this, and I am hungry . . . but what I'm really hungry for can't be sated right now."

He grinned devilishly, obviously picking up on my meaning. "Soon, Dar," he replied quietly, leaning closer. "Just as soon as we figure out what happened to you, we'll fix it and then I'm making you *mine.*"

I shivered and felt thankful for my body's intrinsic response to him. Nothing like a large drop-dead gorgeous werewolf sitting across the table to take one's mind off the fact that one's hands had turned into deadly weapons.

Logan picked up his fork, and he inhaled. A soft glow filled the ring around his irises. I knew it wasn't the breakfast scents he was inhaling.

Thankfully, Cecile and Mike were none the wiser for the hormonal reaction occurring only yards away from them. Cecile busied herself with the schedule as she paced the bus.

"Only twelve clients are on the roster today, which means it will be an easy day," she said when she paced by us. "And only a few days to go before your tour ends." Cecile brought the tip of her pencil to her mouth before she jotted down a few notes. "Tomorrow we'll be in

Spokane, then Kennewick, and our last stop will be just outside of Seattle. Forty-seven more clients to see, Dar."

I forced a forkful of eggs into my mouth. *Forty-seven.* I had forty-seven more lives to save before I could venture to the community and pursue answers to explain the dark power inside me.

Cecile walked back up the aisle, humming along to the music as she scanned the schedule.

"Where are you seeing people today?" Logan asked after Cecile settled on the couch at the front of the bus.

I shrugged. "We rented a room at some random motel. Since this area is remote, it was the only location we could find."

One thing had changed in my tours recently—we no longer needed to hide. Thanks to Logan and the supernatural community, my biological father's memory of me had been wiped clean. Less than a month before, I'd lived in terror that he would kill me. That was before I'd known the stalker who'd threatened my life also shared my blood. Now, deep sadness filled me every time I thought about him. My own father had hurt me, and he'd done it all for money.

"Aren't you going to finish eating?" Logan frowned as he took in my expression. His forearm rested on the table, and his chocolate-brown eyes stared at me with such intensity that I could have sworn he could see into me.

I picked up my fork again, grumbling internally at my oscillating emotions. If I wasn't perving over my boyfriend, I was worrying about my show, stressing about my powers, or feeling sad about my asshole Dad.

Too bad I couldn't spend all of my time perving. That would have been preferable.

"I'm getting full. Do you want to finish mine?"

Logan had already finished his huge breakfast. One thing I'd learned about werewolves—they ate a lot.

"You eat it. You need to keep your strength up for your show." That groove had settled between his eyes again. "Are you worried about it? Is that why you're not eating?"

"A little." I forked a bite of eggs into my mouth and changed subjects since the fluttering had started in my belly again. "Say, has there been any news from Wes about the rogues?"

"Yeah, I got a message from him this morning. They found where Niles lived. A small town about fifty miles north of Silver City, but we're still not sure where Zach lived."

I forced myself to swallow as all pervy thoughts fled when reality set in. As much as I wanted to forget my situation, there was no running from what had happened the previous night. "That's not normal, right? That Niles lived so far away from Jayden and they were working together?"

"No. It's not normal at all."

"Has there been any sign of Zach?"

"At the moment, no. He's disappeared."

I dropped my fork and wrapped my arms around myself. "And the red eyes? Or that smell you said they had that wasn't like other rogue werewolves? Has there been anything found about that? And what about S? Do you know who he is?"

Logan shook his head. "Wes has gone to the courts to request a scholar or two if we can get them. He's hoping the history books will reveal clues about the red eyes and that smell. And to answer your question about S—no. There are over fifty thousand supes in the world with a name starting with *S*. Considering that's all we have to go on, it's not much."

Logan shifted, the bench squeaking. I made myself pick up my fork again. My next show started in a few hours, and Logan was right, I needed to keep my strength up.

"But we'll get to the bottom of this, Dar."

"I hope so. Because, you know, the . . ." I waved at my abdomen. The dark power still swirled inside me, its coldness humming as though it were a life force of its own. "This new power is still in me. I can feel it, and I don't know what to do about it." My breath caught in my throat as a deep chasm of despair opened up inside me.

My hand shook when I tried to spear my eggs, but it was no use. I set my fork down and brought my gaze to his. "I'm scared, Logan," I said quietly. "I don't know what's wrong with me."

His jaw locked, and he automatically reached across the table to touch me but stopped himself at the last moment.

The muscle ticked in his jaw when he said, "We'll figure it out. I promise."

# Chapter 9

"Right this way." Cecile led my first client into the motel room. Noise from the nearby interstate fluttered into the small space until Cecile closed the door firmly behind him.

The man appeared to be in his sixties. Salt-and-pepper hair covered his head, and his tanned complexion made me think he spent a lot of time in the sun. A ready smile filled his lips when he saw me.

For all intents and purposes, he looked healthy, and if it weren't for the hypertrophied legs that draped listlessly in his wheelchair, I would have assumed he was.

"Daria Gresham, it's a pleasure to meet you!" He wheeled himself toward me, the wheels squeaking, then held out his hand. "I'm Connor Jacobson."

"Hi, Connor." I smiled warmly but eyed his hand anxiously.

Cecile hurried in front of me. "Daria avoids touch since it activates her gift. I'm sure you understand."

He dropped his arm. "Oh, of course." He grinned again, and some of my anxiety over the healing session lessened. Connor had an openness about him that few had.

According to Cecile, Connor had requested to see me for an old injury that he'd had most of his life. An accident in his youth had left him paralyzed from the waist down.

Cecile gestured toward the bed. Only the three of us occupied the space since Mike and Logan waited on the bus, so we had plenty of room. "We'll have you lie there while Daria works her gift. Do you need help onto the mattress?"

Connor shook his head. "Oh no, I'll be just fine. I've had forty-two years to learn how to move, but after today, I'll be walking again." Hope and happiness lit his eyes, reminding me of children on Christmas morning.

A few minutes later, Connor was situated on the bed, and Cecile had drawn the curtains. Calming scents of lavender and rosemary from the multiple candles burning on the dresser and nightstand filled the room. The traffic noise faded into the background as I positioned myself at Connor's side.

I lifted my hands. "I'm about to begin, and once I do, it's important that you stay absolutely still and don't interrupt me. Once my gift starts to work, you'll feel its heat, but it won't burn you. It will heal you."

Connor grinned. "I'm ready."

Closing my eyes, I focused on my healing light. When I cracked the lid on the storage chest below my navel, my light sprang forth, winding up my belly and into my arms. Bursts of pain followed, but I ignored that. I was used to my healing sessions hurting me.

The dark power shifted, too, but I tried to focus on the feel of my hands as they warmed.

Standing lightly on the balls of my feet, I shifted and swayed, letting my light tell me exactly where Connor's injury lay. Sickness spiraled around Connor's spinal column, alerting me to his old injury.

I scrunched my eyes tightly closed, concentrating harder than I normally did since the dark power was still swirling in my belly, but I wasn't touching Connor, which made it possible to keep the dark power from hurting him, but still, it was hard.

After taking a deep breath, I dipped my healing light into Connor's body, feeling for the source of his injury. *There.* A satisfied smile spread across my face when I located where the spinal cord was severed. I slid my light away from the decay around his cord and assessed the rest of his body.

My hands moved back and forth, telling me of every ailment that plagued him. He had a few narrowed arteries from atherosclerosis, and thinning muscles in his abdominal wall, leaving him vulnerable to a hernia, but other than that, barely any sickness filled his body.

I shifted my light back to the lumbar area, intending to correct his clogged arteries and thin abdominal muscles at the end of our session.

I worked my light into his spinal column. The exertion caused sweat to bead on my forehead. As my healing light transferred his sickness to me, my legs weakened.

Healing paralyzed clients could prove tricky since during the process I eventually transferred their injury entirely to myself, but Cecile was ready. She'd already moved a chair behind me, the brush of the chair's wooden legs making the barest whisper as she positioned it, ready for my fall.

Concentrating more to avoid any further injury to his spine, I called more upon my light.

The dark power rushed upward.

My eyes flashed open. Connor was lying completely still, his eyes closed while his arms rested at his sides. I took a few shallow breaths, panic filling me.

Cecile watched me from the edge of the room, wrinkles appearing between her eyes as she frowned.

I smiled shakily and licked my dry lips as I tried to reassure myself that it had been a fluke. I wasn't touching Connor. The dark power had only responded before when I'd been touching someone.

*But you've only been living with this power for a day. Who's to say it's actually limited to only touching people? Your light heals without touching people.*

But I pushed that worrying thought aside and hovered my hands above Connor. Taking a deep breath, I closed my eyes again until warmth filled my palms as my healing resumed.

I focused on the calming scents of the candles, using their subtle fragrances to ground my concentration.

*Breathe in, breathe out, Dar. You got this.*

Shifting my hands over his spinal area again, I called forth more light to wrap around his spine, threading together the damaged nerves and strengthening his weak muscles.

My light billowed up inside me like a golden painful glowing ribbon. It trailed down my arms to my hands, making heat shoot from my palms. My worry eased as the healing session resumed.

A second ticked by, then another. My relief grew. Things felt normal, painful but purposeful, like they usually did. *Everything's fine.*

I dug into my healing light again, calling more forth, while I readied myself to transfer his paralysis entirely to my body. *Just a little more light.*

The dark power rushed up again, shooting down my arms like a torpedo.

I shrieked.

The burst of power came from nowhere, and the rush of it was so forceful that I jumped back just as red light shot from my fingertips.

Connor's eyes flashed open as the red power singed the bed beside him, burning the bed and leaving a huge black crater. He pulled away from where the power had landed with a horrified look.

"What was that?" Terror filled his eyes as he looked frantically around the room. He reached over his chest and brushed his arm. Singed hairs sizzled on his skin. "I'm burned!"

I panted, my thighs pressing against the chair that had been ready for my fall. I tried to back up more but stumbled when my foot caught on the chair's leg.

"What's going on?" Connor asked. "I still can't feel my legs."

I gripped my hands tightly together, panic welling up in my chest at what I'd almost done. Cecile kept her distance, for the first time in my life, looking too frightened to approach me.

"I'm sorry," I said, my voice shaking. "I'm so sorry. I didn't mean for that to happen!" I looked down at my trembling hands. They no longer felt safe and familiar. If that power had hit his chest, it would have stopped his heart.

*I'm a killer. I'm still a killer!*

Horror at what I'd become swirled inside me as I shoved my healing power into the well below my navel. I tried to do the same with the dark power, but when I tried to push it, it trembled and felt eager, as if beckoning me to use it. I flinched away from it, no longer trying to control it. Touching it internally and acknowledging it, only seemed to make it grow stronger.

"I'm so sorry!" I whispered again before I ran from the room.

∞   ∞   ∞

I walked at a frantic pace on the highway's shoulder, the gravel from the county road cutting into my thin-soled canvas shoes. Cool wind whipped against my bare legs. Since the hour was early, the day's heat hadn't set in.

With each step, my calf burned, reminding me of my still-healing werewolf bite.

At least ten minutes had gone by since I'd fled the healing session, and as the road passed beneath me, I felt more and more panicked.

*I can't heal people anymore. I can't touch them or use my light on them!*

My new reality was nothing like what my life used to be. At least then, I'd been able to live among others without fear of hurting them—even if their touch hurt *me*.

I was so caught up in my thoughts that I barely heard the footsteps tapping quietly behind me.

Halting abruptly, I twirled around.

Logan stopped several yards away, his hands stuffed into his pockets, a stricken expression on his face. He'd probably been following me the entire time, but I'd been so consumed with grief that I hadn't known it.

The sun played off his dark hair, making some of the strands appear blackish-bronze. He still wore jeans and a T-shirt, but for the first time since I'd met him, I didn't feel a hint of desire.

Only shame.

Shame at what I'd become and regret at what we could never be.

"Did Cecile tell you?" I called hoarsely. Wind washed over my cheeks as tears threatened to stream down my face. "Did you hear what I did? Do you know that I almost killed that man back there?"

His stricken expression remained. He nodded solemnly, his Adam's apple bobbing when he swallowed. "I heard, but it's not your fault, Dar. You would never hurt someone intentionally. It was an accident."

"An accident that almost killed someone!" I turned

away from him and wrapped my arms around myself.

Montana's wild beauty stretched all around me. Cattle lowed in the distance. A small creek cut through the surrounding fields, and mountains rose from the earth like grassy pyramids that touched the sky.

"I can't work anymore," I whispered. "My entire purpose for being on this earth was destroyed in a single event last night. If I can't trust myself and my power, I can't heal people. The entire purpose of my family will die with me. I'll be the reason the Gresham legacy becomes broken."

The weight of the responsibility I'd felt my whole life, the need to perform, to sacrifice certain aspects of my life to fulfill my destiny, all came crashing down on me.

I sank to the ground, the sharp gravel cutting into my butt. When I lifted my hands to my face, small palms and narrow fingers stared back at me. I flipped them over. A few freckles smattered the backs of my hands, and neatly trimmed nails adorned my fingertips, yet inside my hands lay something else—a new power, a new darkness.

And it wasn't something I could control.

"What do I do?" I asked more to myself than him.

Logan approached slowly and sat down a few feet away. Seeing him put extra distance between us only made the pain in my heart grow.

As if sensing my distress, he inched closer, his jeans scraping along the gravel. "Dar, we'll find a way to stop whatever's happening to you. We'll find answers to explain it, then we'll stop it."

I lifted my eyes to his. Surprisingly, the tears stayed at bay. Instead, a deep numbness sank in. "Nobody can help me."

"You don't know that." Logan swallowed, the sound audible above the bubbling creek in the field. "Somebody in the community may be able to help. Maybe the scholars can dig something up."

I cocked my head, the numbness stretching across my chest. I wanted to believe him. I wanted to jump up and run headfirst toward Boise and hope that it could all go away.

But I had a feeling it wouldn't be that easy.

# Chapter 10

Cecile canceled the rest of my shows. With each call she made, the numbness in me grew. Despite lying on my bunk in the back of the bus, I still heard my clients' protests, their anger, their absolute despair that I couldn't save them. They had counted on me.

For most of my clients, I was their last hope. They'd tried everything modern medicine had to offer and hadn't found help. Only my healing light could save them.

"Yes, yes, I know that Mikey's been on the waiting list for eight months," Cecile said to the twentieth client she called. "I know. I know that your child is dying from cancer and that the chemo isn't working . . ."

I squeezed my eyes tightly shut.

We were still parked outside the motel. Connor had

left in his handicap van after I'd fled the room. He would most likely spend the rest of his days in that wheelchair unless a miracle in modern medicine happened and his spinal column could be repaired.

"Yes, of course," Cecile's voice carried to me again. "We'll be sure to let you know as soon as Daria starts working again."

*As soon as . . . If only that were true.*

"Babe?" Logan's quiet voice reached my ears.

I rolled over to face the aisle. His worry-filled gaze assessed me. My bunk being on the top meant we were almost at eye-level.

"We're going to have some lunch before we head to Boise. Do you want to join us?"

A part of me wanted to shake my head and tell him that I wasn't hungry, that eating felt impossible, but then I remembered what my mom and my nan had told me.

*"We're Greshams. Our family has faced hardships for centuries. There will be times in your life when you'll want to give up, where you'll want to crawl into a ball and disappear, but remember why you're here. You carry blood that was meant to heal. Your purpose is to save. Don't let those hardships win. Remember who you are."*

I closed my eyes, remembering their words and their love.

For a fraction of a second, the numbness abated.

*Remember who you are.*

I held on to that growing sense of purpose, the one that had been drummed into me for as long as I could remember.

*I won't forget, Mom, and I won't let you down. I'll find a way to beat this dark power, and I'll reclaim the purpose that our family has lived for. I promise.*

Keeping that thought firmly in place, I pushed up on my elbows and slid out of my bunk. My lips thinned as I straightened my shirt. "Yeah, let's eat then get moving. How far away is Boise?"

A small smile curved Logan's lips. He lifted his hand, his finger reaching for the stray lock of hair across my cheek, but he dropped it at the last second. Still, his smile remained.

"There's that fighting spirit I admire so much. And we're about six hours from Boise. We should be there by evening."

∞ ∞ ∞

We arrived in Boise just after supper. Flat, dry land surrounded the interstate, and in the distance, mountains lined the horizon in gentle mounds. We got off I-84 and drove toward the city center, my nose pressed to the window the entire way, as if I were hoping I would see a sign of magical existence on every street corner we passed.

"Where are the headquarters located?" I glanced over my shoulder to make eye contact with Logan.

He lounged on the couch across from me, his legs stretching across the aisle as he propped his bare feet on my sofa.

I perched on the edge of the cushion and admired his strong frame. A tingle of desire ran through me at the sight of his strong body sprawled out.

That desire brought a sense of relief too. Already, I felt my old self returning. The hours that morning and early afternoon, when despair had wanted to claim me, were disappearing like a bad dream upon waking.

His nostrils flared, a knowing look in his eyes.

*Damn, he's sexy.* I then rolled my eyes internally. There I went, perving again.

"Headquarters are on the north side of the city, near the foothills. Our location is hidden in plain sight from the humans."

I dropped back onto the couch, eliciting a twinge of pain in my calf. "Hidden in plain sight?"

"A cloaking spell keeps us completely hidden, similar to what Holly did back at the park but on a much vaster scale. When we enter the headquarters, we have to access a special portal. Only supernatural blood and an SF security pass allow admittance."

I cocked my head. "So what do humans see when you enter the portal?"

"Nothing. They'd see us walking along as if we never stopped."

"Seriously?"

A smile stretched across his face. "Seriously. On top of the witches' cloaking spell, the entire headquarters is warded and guarded with sorcerer magic. Once we drive on to the warded road, if a human is watching, they'll see the bus continuing on. However, we'll actually stop to get out so that we can enter headquarters. When we do that, an illusion is created, making it seem as if we simply kept driving."

I crossed my legs beneath me, my interest in the

passing scenery forgotten. "But what if a human follows us in their own car? Wouldn't they notice the bus stopping?"

"No, they wouldn't. The illusion would make it look like the bus continued driving and never stopped. That's why we use sorcerer magic since they can manipulate memory and thought patterns. Even if a human were following the magical illusion of the bus, eventually their attention would wane. They would forget that a bus had ever been in front of them, so when the illusion ends the human would carry on driving, none the wiser to having their thought patterns altered by a sorcerer."

"That's amazing. So is it like a magical fog around the SF headquarters or something?"

"No, it's a barrier. You'll see exactly what I mean when we get there. Once you cross the barrier's threshold, if you're human, you're sensitive to the spells the sorcerers and witches have weaved. And once you get to the end of the barrier and leave it, your memory's altered—again, only if you're human."

I shook my head, stunned at how much I still didn't know. "Incredible."

"What's incredible?" Cecile asked, walking toward us from the back of the bus.

"Just stuff about the community that Logan's been telling me." I scooted over on the couch so she could sit beside me.

Cecile sat only a few inches away. She didn't seem as wary as she'd been in the motel room with Connor the day before. "It sounds like this city is full of magic."

Logan scratched his chin. "It is, yet none of the

humans living here even know it."

I eyed Cecile then Mike, who was following the directions Logan had given him. We were less than twenty minutes away from headquarters.

"So what happens to Cecile and Mike when we get there?" I frowned, suddenly realizing that my only family left in the world was subject to the very magic Logan had described.

"Nothing, initially. They'll be able to see when we get out, and they'll see when we walk toward headquarters, but after we step through the portal, the illusion is created. Even though we disappear, they'll see us still walking, and after they drive away, they won't remember having seen us at all."

Cecile's eyebrows rose. "We won't?"

Logan shook his head. "You'll remember dropping Daria and me off somewhere, but you won't be able to find the exact spot again even if your life depended on it."

She frowned. "Then how in the world will we find you again?"

Logan grinned. "You won't. We'll find you."

∞   ∞   ∞

The sun dipped closer to the horizon when we reached the northern foothills. The fading light bathed the fields and rolling hills in a reddish gold, but as we drove deeper into the foothills, the vegetation grew. Dry brown grass swayed in the wind, and various pine species, hemlock, and western red cedars dominated the landscape, rising alongside the narrow two-lane road, making it seem as if we were traveling through a tunnel.

"Looks like a nice place to go for a hike," I commented.

Logan winked. "Or a run."

Smiling, I rolled my eyes. "I'm guessing you mean a four-legged run, not a two-legged one?"

"Good guess." He chuckled. "It's not too much farther, about a hundred yards. Do you see the barrier?"

I rose and walked closer to the front of the bus to peer out the windshield. At first, I didn't see anything, but when I squinted and leaned down, the barrier appeared.

My jaw dropped. A fine, glowing red ribbon stretched across the road before it disappeared in the trees alongside the highway. It waved and shimmered, as if manipulated by the wind, but I doubted nature's elements affected it.

Logan's heavy footsteps came from behind me, then came Cecile's.

"Do you see it now?" he asked, hunkering down to be at eye level with me. His scent fluttered my way, making my head spin.

Taking a deep breath, I ignored the delicious tingles that shot down my spine at how near he stood. "Yeah, I see it."

I marveled at the barrier again, wondering how my mother, my nan, and I would have reacted a year ago if we'd driven up this road by chance, especially when Cecile and Mike wouldn't have been able to see it. We hadn't known about the supernatural community then.

Cecile frowned. "What do you see? I don't see anything."

I stepped forward. "What about you, Mike?"

He just shrugged, his hands casually holding the wheel. "Uh, nope, nothing, Dar. Just a road, trees, and grass."

But to me it was so much more than that. Magic surrounded this part of the world. The closer we got to the barrier, the more I sensed it.

"It has a flavor," I said, turning to Logan. "Like mint, with a hint of . . ." I paused then caught a subtle, bitter taste. "And anise."

Logan smiled, his straight white teeth bright in contrast with his tanned face. "That's right. Not all supernaturals can taste it. Only those with strong abilities can pick up a sorcerer's magical taste." His pleased look remained. "You're truly something, Miss Gresham."

I ducked my head, embarrassed by his praise but also holding on to the belief that all hope wasn't lost for my future. My magic was still strong. Maybe, just maybe, I would be strong enough to beat the dark power that flowed turbulently alongside my healing light.

After all, I was about to enter the Supernatural Forces headquarters, the next day I would see where some of the community resided, and within twenty-four hours, Logan and I would be actively searching for a way to rid me of whatever had awoken inside me. And seeing and tasting that billowy magical barrier that grew brighter the closer we got made a solution seem more possible, even probable.

My grin grew.

"You can stop here," Logan called to Mike.

Mike applied the brakes, and the bus slowed as it

drifted to the road's shoulder, before coming to a complete halt. Mike pulled his Yankees cap off and threw it on the dash. "This is it?" he asked dubiously.

"This is it." Logan grabbed the small bag that he'd brought along when he'd flown from California. "Dar?" He held out his hand to me but dropped it at the last second and clenched it into a fist.

I watched his muscled arm fall back to his side, wishing I could have taken his outstretched hand. *Soon. Just as soon as we figure out what the hell is wrong with me.*

I reached for my backpack which held a few days' worth of clothes. After I slung it over my shoulders, I opened my purse to make sure my cell phone was in it. "Will my phone work in there?"

"Yeah, all human electronics still work normally, but every now and then, reception is spotty. But that's only if the sorcerers are strengthening the barrier."

"Uh, okay. That's reassuring." I zippered my purse and turned to Cecile. "I guess we'll see you soon."

"Take care, Dar," Cecile replied.

We'd already decided that I would spend the next few nights inside the headquarters with Logan. Since it was where Logan normally lived, it was his home, but humans weren't usually allowed in. According to Logan, only the most powerful sorcerer could help a human pass through the portal, and that was only done in extreme circumstances.

I draped my purse over my shoulder and grabbed my jacket from the couch.

Cecile and Mike both stood and watched us step out of the bus. Once we were outside, the flavor of the sorcerer's magic increased, and the barrier glowed only yards away.

"The entry portal's right over there." Logan waved toward a bare patch of grass just off the road.

My eyes widened. The portal's arched red doorway glowed. It rose about seven feet from the ground and spread three feet wide. I hesitated but then told myself it was silly to be nervous.

I gripped my purse firmly to my side and made sure my backpack's straps were tight before striding forward, Logan at my side.

"I'd hold your hand through the portal if I could." He raked a hand through his hair, the wind ruffling his dark-brown locks. "The first time is always a little . . . jarring."

"It's okay. I'm ready."

Logan shouldered his duffel bag. "Come stand beside me. If we both step through at the same time, we'll come out at the same time too."

I brushed closer to his side, wishing more than anything that I could touch him.

He flattened his palm against a glowing area by the portal door. Magic enveloped his hand, glittering around his palm before a pink light emitted from the portal to scan his face.

"Welcome, Logan Smith and guest," a quiet robotic voice said.

The entire portal began to shimmer. Whereas before it had simply been a glowing red ribbon outlining a door, the inside turned opaque, as if a pearly soup.

Logan grinned. "Ready?"

"As ready as I'll ever be."

"On the count of three. One . . . two . . . three."
We simultaneously stepped forward.

# Chapter 11

Wind screeched in my ears. Next came the feeling of being stretched to the point of my bones snapping, but just as those sensations exploded—they stopped.

The spinning world around me came to a halt. Blood whooshed through my ears, and my heart pounded. I gasped quietly, gulping in a lungful of air.

"Dar?" Logan asked.

It was only then that I realized I'd closed my eyes. I opened them hesitantly, and his grinning face came into view.

"Are you okay?"

I took a deep breath and felt frantically for my purse and my backpack. They still hung from my shoulders. *Weird.* The journey through the portal had made everything feel like it was ripping apart, yet my clothes and my bags were fully intact. I threaded my fingers through my hair anyway, embarrassment flooding my cheeks.

"Ah, yeah, I'm fine." I surveyed the room we stood in. Grayish metallic paint covered the walls, and bright artificial light illuminated the enclosed space. Nobody else was around.

Logan grinned more. "You did great. Most people either have a panic attack or are screaming when they emerge from the portal the first time."

I grimaced. "Well . . . I can see why. It was kind of terrifying." My heart still beat like a wild drum, but as each moment passed, it slowed more.

"Don't worry. You'll get used to it."

A robotic voice suddenly rang from . . . somewhere. It didn't sound like it came from any certain area, more that it came from *everywhere*. "Welcome, Logan Smith and guest. Please proceed to the identification processing room."

"Processing room?" I raised an eyebrow.

"It's required of everyone who enters the headquarters. We need to check in, but then I can show you around. As you can see, we're in the entry bay right now. Now follow me. We gotta go this way." He nodded over his shoulder and lifted his duffel bag. He strode forward, the familiar swagger of his hips beckoning my attention as his shoulders strained against the weight of his bag. Even in a new place filled with endless curiosities, all I could think about was how incredibly sexy he was.

I followed Logan from the room into a hallway.

Similar to the entry bay, it was composed of gray walls and a concrete floor. In a way, the headquarters felt like a bunker or a military base.

"Are we underground?" I searched for a window but didn't see one, but as we traveled down the tunnel, voices drifted to me from ahead.

"No. There are subterranean levels, but this area is aboveground. The entry bay and the processing area are all enclosed, though. That's why there are no windows around here. You know, in case someone tried to break in through the portal—that way, they'd be contained and unable to escape by breaking a window, unless they carried personal portal keys. Then walls wouldn't contain them."

"Oh, right." *Maybe someday I'll actually know what he's talking about.*

Our feet tapped quietly on the floor as we proceeded down the hallway. A few steps later, we entered a large bustling room. At least a dozen people appeared busy at work. The circular room held an impressive workstation around its perimeter. Several technicians sat in front of computers and holographic screens.

In the center of the room, a holographic display flashed brilliant colors and showed various areas of the world. The images constantly changed, glimmering from city to city as beacons lit up and identified individuals.

An image appeared in the flashing display, showing a female with short blond hair walking in what appeared to be a European city. Cobblestones lined the path, and her three-inch heels showcased her graceful walk. A watery canal glimmered next to the narrow road, while old buildings no more than two stories high lined the other side.

A glowing screen popped up above her. *Emily M. Sanders—witch, 5'5", 140 lbs. Current location—Amsterdam. Day four of mission—pursuing a rumor of six nested vampires reported in the Amsterdam area.*

Logan nodded toward the screen. "That's how we keep track of SF members. We're all continually tracked by headquarters in case we run into any trouble."

"Logan!"

I twirled around at the sound of a familiar voice.

Brodie strode toward us, grinning. "Look who the cat dragged in." He winked at me and stepped closer, his arm out, as if he were going to shoulder hug me.

I flinched back, acutely aware of the dark power humming inside me. "I didn't know you'd be here, Brodie, but best not to get too close."

He cocked his head then shrugged in that nonchalant way of his.

He looked exactly as I remembered him: blond hair, sparkling blue eyes, and lips that always tilted up, hinting that a smart comment or sarcastic quip could erupt from his mouth at any moment.

Brodie put his hands on his hips and turned toward Logan. "The boys and I are back from California."

A surprised expression filled Logan's face. "Does that mean you figured out who stole Xanthia's dragon?"

Brodie shook his head. "Hell no. We brought her back with us. She's stopped her part-time dragon-training gig to officially jump back onto SF payroll. It's going to take more than a few weeks and the five of us to figure this one out."

"If she's on the SF payroll, does that mean she works for the SF too?" I asked.

"Yeah." Brodie shoved his hands into his pockets. "Xanthia's half demon, which means she can travel between the realms. The SF has quite a few half demons on staff for that exact purpose. Normally, Xanthia doesn't do SF work, though. She lives in Cali when she's not training dragons, but when we need help with underworld stuff, she'll jump in—hence, her part-time status."

Most of what Brodie had said to me made zero sense, but before I could ask him to explain more, a woman approached us.

"Hello, you must be Daria Gresham." An SF uniform covered her plump build. Cherub cheeks lifted when she smiled, pink hair curled around her heart-shaped face, and her inquisitive hazel eyes met mine. "I was hoping to be on duty when you arrived."

Logan gestured toward her. "Daria, this is Millie, one of our resident fairies and part of the SF processing team."

*A fairy?* I tried not to look too eager to meet another supernatural species. "Nice to meet you, Millie."

Millie tucked a strand of her pink hair behind her ear, revealing the top of the pointy appendage. Other than that, she looked like a human, although her skin held a subtle glow. I wondered if she was anything like the fairies portrayed in fairytales, but considering her warm and welcoming demeanor, I guessed not.

"I hear that you had some trouble with your father a few weeks ago." Millie raised an eyebrow.

"Yeah, that's right, but Logan and his friends helped with that."

"Along with a few of our sorcerers." Millie winked. "I met your father when Douglas worked on him. Your father wasn't . . ." She tapped her chin. "How do I put this . . . very pleasant?" She laughed, the sound reminding me of a thousand tinkling bells. "But he won't be bothering you anymore."

I gripped my purse again, not wanting to dwell on any memories of my father.

"Anyway, I better do my job before I get in trouble." She pulled out a tablet from her pocket. The sleek device looked similar to the tablet Wes had typed on the other day. "Do you mind holding your wrist out?"

I tensed.

Logan leaned down and said quietly, "It's just a scan. Don't worry. She won't touch you."

Relaxing, I straightened my arm, and Millie pointed the tablet at my exposed skin. Lasers erupted from the device. Following that, a warm, tingling sensation grew in my wrist. My eyes widened when a glowing symbol appeared on my skin before it disappeared.

"A witch, just as we suspected." She holstered her tablet again. "All checked in."

I flipped my arm up and down, searching for whatever she'd done to me.

"You can't see it," Brodie said, "but you've been tagged. Consider your privacy now obsolete."

My eyes widened so much I was sure they resembled saucers.

Brodie laughed. "Just kidding. That little tag merely

verifies your supernatural species and that you are who you say you are. The witches came up with that one. It detects anybody who's attempting to mask their appearance or identity. But don't worry." He grinned again, his eyes twinkling. "You passed with flying colors. You are indeed Daria Gresham, and you are indeed a witch."

"But how do you know that?"

"If you weren't, the symbol would have branded you and not disappeared. Then we could hunt you down." He nodded toward the center holographic column.

I gulped. "Oh. Right."

Logan held out his arm next, and Millie did the same to him. When she finished, the hush in the room finally caught my attention. Everybody who had been working on the computers had stopped to watch us.

Millie leaned closer to me, and I instinctively jumped back. The dark power still coiled in my belly, ready to strike. However, she didn't react to my skittishness and merely whispered, "You better get used to it. You're a bit of a celebrity in the community, you know."

"I am?"

Millie just winked.

Logan eyed Brodie. "So why did things never get sorted out in California?"

The teasing look in Brodie's eyes disappeared. He crossed his arms over his chest, his biceps bulging. Similar to Logan, he was huge.

"I think the problem goes deeper than someone tampering with hell's gatekeepers."

I cocked my head. *Hell's gatekeepers?*

Logan's brow furrowed as those around us turned back to their computers. "Are Jake and Alexander here too?"

"Yeah, they're in the gym, shooting some hoops."

"Well, gentlemen . . ." Millie mockingly bowed and took a step back. "I'll let you get to it, so you can show the lovely Daria around." Her full lips parted into a smile, revealing rows of pointy teeth. She turned her smile on me. "I hope to see you around. I'd love to get to know you better."

I tried not to stare at her teeth. "Yeah, I'm sure I'll see you around."

"Dar? This way." Logan nodded toward another hall that exited the circular room. From the looks of it, four different hallways branched out from the processing area. One of them led to our entry bay. "I'll show you around first since I'm guessing you're curious, then we can touch base with Wes to see if the scholars have any ideas about your newly acquired skill."

"Skill?" Brodie cocked his head.

"It's a long story," I said hastily. The fewer people that knew about my lethal power, the better. The last thing I wanted to do was make everyone terrified to be around me. So far, I hadn't had any strange power outbursts, other than that one healing session, and from the little I'd learned about the dark power inside me, it only acted up when I called upon my light or when I was afraid.

Hopefully, it would stay that way.

"How big is this place?" I asked when we entered a new hallway.

Brodie shrugged. "The building itself sits on two acres and has two levels above ground and two levels below ground. But the surrounding land is around fifty thousand acres. We like to have enough room to stretch our legs." He waggled his eyebrows.

I snorted quietly. I was pretty sure he was referring to four furry legs, not two human ones. "And you all live here too?"

"Yep, in the barracks." Brodie stretched his arms wide. "Home sweet home. Maybe I can show you my digs." He winked, getting a laugh out of me.

"You still love trying to charm my girlfriend, don't you?" Logan's tone sounded irritated, but I caught the amused tilt of his lips.

Brodie gave a satisfied grunt. "Trying? Pretty sure I'm not trying. She loves me." He nudged my shoulder, making me jump, but our contact broke quickly. "Admit it. You think I'm dashingly handsome and way more charming than this oaf."

"I suppose you're just as handsome."

Logan laughed just as Brodie brought a hand to his chest. "Ouch. You seriously think this dude's more charming than me?"

I smiled. "Just kidding, Brodie. You're not only handsome but also quite charming."

He grinned, a new swagger in his step. "Exactly as I thought."

Logan rolled his eyes, but a twinkle still lit them.

I followed the two of them down the hall. At our next turn, natural light poured into the hall from ahead. When the first window appeared, I eagerly looked out of it.

Rolling hills and thick forest carpeted the landscape. I craned my neck, trying to see some of the houses that had been along the road during the drive in, but couldn't see any.

"Are there any homes or farms around here?" I propped my arm on the windowsill.

"No. Not in the immediate area." Logan came closer to my side. A whiff of his tantalizing scent drifted my way.

My head swam. I wished I could step closer and lean against him. As if responding to my unbidden desire, the dark power churned within me. I hastily took a step farther away from Logan and again tried to push it into the chest where I stored my light.

I grumbled quietly. It *still* wouldn't budge.

Logan continued talking, forcing my attention back to my surroundings.

"The magical barrier deters potential land seekers or hunters, and even if somebody *did* wander into this area, despite the sorcerer's magic, they wouldn't see any of our buildings or any of us, even if we were walking around in the middle of the day."

"Is that witch magic?" I asked.

He nodded. "Combine the witches' cloaking spells with the sorcerers' deterrent and mind spells, and we have a perfectly hidden location in plain sight."

"Would *we* see humans walking around here even though they couldn't see us?" I glanced Logan's way, taking in the hard edge of his jaw and his aquiline profile. *I wish I could touch him.* Sometimes, he was so beautiful, he took my breath away.

"Yeah, we would see them, if that were to happen, which it rarely does," Logan replied.

"So what happens if a human does walk here?"

"We send out whichever sorcerer is on the clock at the time to deter them. That usually works like a charm."

I smiled cheekily up at him. "No pun intended."

Logan grinned, seeming to enjoy my newfound lightheartedness.

Brodie snickered. "Any encounter with a sorcerer completely messes with a human's head. According to Douglas, the last time anyone made the poor choice to come near this facility, they had a headache for three days straight and had nightmares anytime they pondered returning to these foothills."

"Sounds like it works pretty well."

I pushed away from the window, and we carried on down the hall.

Logan and Brodie showed me the various areas of the Supernatural Forces headquarters. Most of the large facility consisted of huge training rooms, outdoor combat areas, shooting ranges in case they used human weapons, and living barracks. Logan informed me that the more top-secret information resided in the lower subterranean levels, and not surprisingly, I wasn't allowed to go down there.

"So where will I be staying for the next few nights?" I asked, shielding my eyes from the setting sun.

We stood outside beside another intricate jungle of ropes, ladders, pits, and walls—all part of a normal day's workout, according to Brodie. The sun's last rays cut through the distant hills as the scent of pine needles carried on the wind.

Logan cocked his head. "In my apartment, of course."

"But you know I can't—" I lowered my voice, hoping Brodie wouldn't hear. "That I can't sleep near you," I whispered.

I knew my embarrassment was silly since I had no control over the dark power, yet I felt inadequate, as if I were a brand-new witch in her infancy trying to learn her powers all over again. The last time I'd felt that inept was when I was ten years old. But try as I might, I still felt as embarrassed as hell.

Logan's gaze didn't waver. "I'll sleep on the floor. Don't worry." He hooked a thumb back toward the main building. "Should we go find Wes?"

I nodded vigorously, and other than a curious tilt of his head, Brodie didn't comment.

Dry wind cut through the trees when we headed back to the large building. Since the facility was so huge, it was strange to think that humans wouldn't be able to see it. The square structure appeared simple yet intimidating. Windows dotted the two stories above ground, and everything else looked hard and concrete, except for the brick barracks behind us, but none of it seemed magical. Headquarters simply looked like a military training facility.

"What do humans see when they look at this?"

Brodie shrugged. "Just fields, grass, and trees. You know, boring stuff."

Once inside, we headed to an elevator. Our feet tapped along the concrete as we traveled down another hallway.

"I need to go down to one of the subterranean levels to get Wes." Logan checked his phone again. "I sent him a message to let him know we arrived, but I haven't heard back yet. He must be caught up in something." He turned toward me, hands on his hips. "Can you stay here and wait for me?" His expression turned apologetic. "I can't take you down there."

"Yeah, I know. I'll stay here."

"Don't worry. I'll keep her company." Brodie waggled his eyebrows.

Logan hit the button on the elevator. "I won't be long, and Brodie, try not to steal my girlfriend."

"You know I don't make promises I can't keep." A buzz sounded from Brodie's pocket. He pulled out his cell phone, and a grin lit up his face. "Speaking of stealing your girlfriend away . . . looks like a few are heading out for the night to hit some of the downtown bars. Want to go? If Wes is busy, it may be a good way to pass time tonight. You can see him first thing tomorrow morning."

My heart jumped into my throat at the thought of being in a crowded bar with intoxicated humans and supernaturals. *If someone were to accidentally brush against me or startle me . . .*

I twisted my hands. "I don't think that's a good idea."

The elevator door dinged open just as Logan shook his head. "Not for us. You go on ahead."

"Seriously?" Brodie's dazzling blue eyes dimmed. "Not even one drink on your first night here?"

"Normally, I'd love to, but . . ." I wrung my hands more.

"Not tonight," Logan said firmly. The pitch of his

voice changed, eliciting goose bumps from me. I'd only heard that tone from him one other time, when I'd overheard Brodie talking about me in a less than flattering way outside Peter's magic shop a few weeks earlier, before I knew Logan and his friends were werewolves.

Brodie immediately stepped back, his head dipping down. "Sure. No problem. I'll catch you guys tomorrow. And, Daria, no running away."

He turned on his heel and disappeared around one of the turns. I cocked my head just as Logan stepped into the elevator. "What just happened?"

He grinned. "Just asserted a little dominance in my tone. It comes in handy at times. Now, wait here, and don't go anywhere, got it? Not even if you hear something weird. Stay put. I'll be back in a minute."

The elevator doors closed, leaving me in the empty hallway. Stunned, I leaned against the wall, shaking my head. I'd just learned another new thing about Logan. Apparently, he was a dominant werewolf. *So what does that mean? Is he an alpha or something?*

I pinched the bridge of my nose. I could add that to my list of growing questions.

As I waited and waited for Logan to return, I readjusted my backpack at least a dozen times and checked my phone twice that many. I had reception but no new messages from Logan.

When twenty minutes passed, I figured he got roped into something. Sighing, I leaned against the wall and slid to the floor. I pulled a book out of my bag and was about to crack it open when a faint yell reached my ears. I straightened.

"Help!"

My eyes widened. The scream was faint, but someone had definitely called for help.

"Please! Please help me!"

I hastily rose from the floor and sprinted in the direction that I'd heard the call.

"Help me!"

I rounded the corner, my feet slapping against the floor, and a twinge from my werewolf bite worked its way up my calf. Commotion sounded behind a pair of double doors at the end of the hall.

I didn't think when I reached them, merely reacted. I wrenched the doors open and flew inside.

An explosion of fiery light assaulted me the second I stepped into the room. Bright, hot magic flowed over my skin and sucked my breath away. I yelped as pain from the magic burned my skin and burrowed into my chest.

Screaming, I sank to the floor, and in that second, when I expected the magic I'd been hit with to kill me, the dark power responded.

A rush of power burst to life inside me and flowed from every pore. The lethal magic I'd been hit with tried to burrow into my heart, but the dark power shielded me. The pain from the magic evaporated as it ricocheted off the darkness, shooting from my chest across the room. Red light tore from my body.

Following that, someone screamed.

# Chapter 12

"Phoenix?" a woman yelled. "No! Shit! Phoenix!"

My breath came out in a rush as my heart pounded. I rose from the floor, my movements sluggish from whatever the hell had just happened to me.

I stood in some kind of warehouse filled with obstacles and training equipment. The lights were dim, making it hard to see, but I watched, stunned, as five men and women rushed toward a fallen man.

All of them wore combat gear and goggles and carried some kind of weapon. One of the women dropped her strange-looking gun, fell to her knees, and cradled the injured man in her lap.

Blood poured from his side, and a deep pit formed in my stomach. *Did I do that?*

"Get help!" the woman screamed.

I backed against the wall just as two men and a woman ran past me and out the door, only one glancing my way on his way out.

My queasiness intensified as I remembered the red light that had shot from me. Blood continued to pour from the man. Once again, the dark power had rushed to my aid. *What have I done?*

"Where's the medic?" the woman yelled. She tore her goggles and helmet off. Long brown hair cascaded down her back, hiding her face from view.

My healing instincts kicked into action. I pushed away from the wall and ran toward them.

Only the woman cradling the man and one other supernatural remained in the room. Both were trying to stop the bleeding coming from the injured man's side, but a dark-red river of blood gushed out despite their best efforts.

I skidded to a stop next to them, quickly assessing the situation. The man lay listlessly, his complexion terrifyingly pale. *He's losing too much blood.*

The woman's head snapped in my direction. "Who the hell are you?" She protectively cradled the injured man to her, as if unsure if I would hurt him again. "Ray?"

The other man, a huge guy with ebony skin, kept one hand on the injured man's side, but he lifted his other hand and muttered a spell. A swirling ball appeared from his palm, ready to strike.

I held up my hands in surrender. "I'm sorry. I'm Daria Gresham. I came through those doors when I heard a call for help. I shouldn't have—" But I stopped talking. We were wasting time, and time was exactly what we didn't have. If I didn't act immediately, the man would die. "Help me get his shirt off." I fell to my knees next to them.

The woman clutched the injured man tighter to her. "Daria Gresham?" She glanced at her comrade.

Ray dropped his hand, and the swirling spell disappeared. He resumed pressing both hands against the man's side, trying to stop the blood again. "She's that healing witch."

"I can save him, but if we don't act now, he will die!" The dark power and my healing light both rushed forward when I called upon my light. It took everything in me to control the dark power and not let it erupt. Sweat popped up on my brow.

The woman's panicked eyes met mine. Maybe it was something in my tone, or maybe it was because nothing she was doing was saving the man, but she gave a curt nod and began removing his combat shirt.

"Let me." Ray mumbled a few words under his breath. The injured man's shirt vanished.

I saw the wound then, a large open gash. "What's his name?" I asked tersely.

"Phoenix," she replied.

Phoenix's lips had already turned blue, and his skin was deathly pale. "Move back, and don't say a word!"

They both scrambled away, letting Phoenix's listless body loll on the floor. I hovered my hands over him and closed my eyes.

A part of me knew that I probably couldn't heal him. The dark power could rush up again and finish what it had started, but if I did nothing, death was inevitable.

*Please! Please work!*

My palms grew hot as I called up my healing light. Pain sparked along my nerves. The dark power wanted to rise, too, but I pushed it down as hard as I could. It took everything in me to try to separate the powers. They both responded, both wanting to do what I asked of them. In a way, they felt like one, but at the moment I only needed my light.

*Stay back! Stay down!* I yelled at the dark power as if it were a poorly trained dog.

My light rushed forward again. More painful shocks from my light made me wince, but I ignored the pain and called upon all of the light I had. It shot down my arms into my hands, the dark power right on its tail. *No! Stay back!*

For a moment, the dark power retreated.

I seized my light while I could. Though I had no idea how long the dark power would stay back, from how eager it felt, I knew it wouldn't be long.

I moved my hands directly over the gushing wound. Phoenix was completely unresponsive, his skin pure white, and a lightning-quick assessment told me that his heart was beating terrifyingly slowly.

"Stay with me, Phoenix."

Heat rushed from my body as sweat erupted from every pore of my skin. I trembled with the amount of energy it took to call my healing light into full action. The dark power still fought me. It still wanted to take over, and I wrestled with it continuously to keep it from dominating my light.

*Extract the injury, Daria. Take it out! Don't let this man die. Don't be responsible for taking another life!*

I felt for Phoenix's collapsed blood vessels then concentrated harder and slowly knit them back together. I pumped my life force into him. At first, his heart didn't respond, but then a steady *lub-dub* resumed. His heart rate picked up as I used my energy to refuel the blood that he'd lost.

My arms trembled more, and sweat slid in a river past my ear. I could feel myself growing weaker. Trauma cases were something I rarely dealt with since they came suddenly, but they required an incredible amount of energy in a short time. The man was only the second actively bleeding victim I'd treated, and I'd certainly never had to contend with the dark power on top of it.

As my healing progressed, I grew weaker. Light poured from me into him as a heavy ache grew in my side at the exact same spot of Phoenix's injury.

*It's working!*

A groan came from Phoenix just as my vision began to blur. The dark power rushed forward.

I yelped and jumped back, moving my hands away from everyone just as red light shot from my fingertips.

A loud explosion came from the floor when the dark power hit it.

"What the hell is going on?" I vaguely registered Logan's yell as footsteps pounded behind me.

Phoenix moaned as I fell back on the floor.

"Babe?" Logan crouched at my side.

But I couldn't open my eyes. I was too tired, and the pain was too great.

"Logan," I whispered. Another groan came from Phoenix just as I lost consciousness.

∞　∞　∞

I awoke to the feel of a soft sheet covering me. My eyelids fluttered open.

"Daria?" Logan lurched forward from his chair and hovered over me. Worry covered his face, etched so deeply in the groove between his eyes that it rivaled the Grand Canyon.

"Logan?" I licked my lips. "Where am I?"

"The healing center." He raked a hand through his hair. "Shit, Dar. You scared the crap out of me."

I tried to sit up from the narrow bed I lay on. I was in a small room, and the lone window revealed a nighttime sky outside, a thousand glittering stars above. "What happened?"

An older woman appeared beside Logan and gently pushed me down until I lay flat. A long flowing robe cascaded around her body, and her kind brown eyes met mine. "Ah, the young Gresham woman has awoken at last." She shooed Logan aside. "I'm Rose and am assigned to your care." She fluttered her fingers over me and murmured a spell.

A soothing feeling settled along my skin, lessening my anxiety. I shook my head. "What the heck is going on? Why am I here?"

"As Logan said, you're in the healing center," Rose replied in a soothing voice. "An event happened earlier in one of the training rooms. From what we can gather, you stopped Phoenix from dying after he shot a hex at you. He thought you were one of the holographic images produced in the training session, not realizing you were a live person."

"An event? He thought I was a holographic image?" Then it all came crashing back—waiting by the elevators for Logan and Wes, hearing the cry for help, rushing through the double doors, and walking into some kind of magical battleground.

I brought a hand to my forehead. "But I heard someone calling for help. That's why I responded! How was I to know they wouldn't realize I was a live person?"

Logan laced his hands together, his expression haggard. "What you heard were illusionary victims in that training scenario. We all know they're not real, so we ignore cries like that from those rooms. It's why I told you to stay put and not go anywhere, no matter what you heard." He rose abruptly, his chair squeaking back. "I should have warned you more clearly before I left. This is entirely my fault." He paced a few steps before he sat back down.

"But what about Phoenix?" I frantically looked toward the closed door. "Where is he?"

"Phoenix is all right. He's in another room, recovering." Rose's serene expression made it seem as if he were healing from a bad cold instead of a deadly magical battle. "It's not the first time he's been injured. He'll be fine." She cocked her head. "But if you hadn't healed him as much as you did, I'm afraid it would be another story. You used your healing magic on him, didn't you?"

"Yeah, I knew if I didn't, he would die." I swallowed sharply. A memory of the dark power taking over during my healing session and how it caused Phoenix's injury rose in my mind. I hung my head. "But if it *wasn't* for me, he never would have been hurt in the first place. I never should have gone in there."

Logan scowled. "That's not your fault. It's *my* fault for not warning you better, and it's *my* fault for taking so long to get back to you." He took a deep breath, the glow around his irises increasing. "It was the dark power that did that to Phoenix, wasn't it?"

My lips trembled.

Rose glanced at Logan then me. "Dark power?"

I ignored her interest and gave Logan the barest hint of a nod.

His mouth tightened into a thin line.

At that moment, the door opened. Wes strode in, followed by Brodie, Jake, Alexander, and the team who had been in the training center.

"That's her!" The woman with the long brown hair raised a finger, pointing at me. "She's the one who almost killed Phoenix!"

Wes stepped forward, deep wrinkles lining his eyes. Like all werewolves, he towered over six feet, but despite his age, steely strength and purpose oozed from him.

"Daria? Is it true? Did you hurt Phoenix?"

I wrung my hands. "It all happened really fast. I—"

"She didn't know about the training rooms," Logan cut in. "It's not her fault."

Wes put his hands on his hips. "I thought you told her to stay where she was."

"I did, but I should have been more clear."

Wes turned his gaze on me. "If Logan told you to remain where you were, why did you enter that training room?"

Humiliation washed through me. In hindsight, I should have heeded Logan's warning.

I hung my head again. "I heard someone calling for help. I thought someone was seriously hurt, and I didn't think. I reacted. I completely forgot that Logan said not to move."

"She almost killed him!" the brown-haired woman yelled.

Wes held up a hand. "Priscilla, I know you're angry, but this sounds like a genuine accident."

Combat gear still covered Priscilla's tall frame, and her lush dark hair looked like a chocolate waterfall down her back. She was truly striking.

Priscilla rounded on Wes. "Who comes here and doesn't know better than to rush headfirst into a training room? Even if she's some famous healing witch?" She threw up her hands. "This is the SF headquarters! Even my five-year-old nephew would know better than that!" She crossed her arms and cast me a scathing look. "*And* she used some kind of magic against us. Something erupted from her, some kind of red light, and it hit Phoenix, nearly killing him, *and* created a hole in the floor. That doesn't seem like something a *healer* would do."

*No, but it's something a killer would do.*

I curled my fingers into the blanket so my hands wouldn't shake.

Logan growled. "Phoenix would have died if it

weren't for Daria. She saved him."

"Yeah," Alexander agreed. "You should be thanking her."

Brodie and Jake murmured their agreement.

Priscilla swirled around, anger exuding from her stance as she confronted the werewolves. "Thank her? Are you fucking kidding me? If it *weren't* for her, he never would have been hit in the first place!"

"His hex hit her first." Logan straightened, his voice rising. "She defended herself, as any of us would have."

Priscilla bristled. "Why is she here, anyway? She's not an SF member. She shouldn't be here, even if she's famous."

I sank farther into the bed, wishing I could disappear beneath it. Logan and I had come to headquarters hoping for help and guidance. Instead, I'd almost killed an innocent SF member within my first hour of arriving, and I had an entire squad of members that apparently hated me and didn't want me there.

"Priscilla's right," Ray said before crossing his arms. His dark skin blended into the night. Biceps as big as Logan's flexed when he held his stance. If I hadn't seen his magic in the training center, I would have assumed he carried werewolf blood. "If Daria hadn't entered that restricted area when she did, none of this would have happened. She ran right into Phoenix's blast." His frown deepened. "Why was she left unattended, anyway? She's not one of us. She shouldn't have been left alone."

The other three supernaturals who'd been training with Ray, Priscilla, and Phoenix—two men and a woman—all watched, not commenting but avidly listening.

The dark power rolled in my belly as fear sprang to life inside me. *They're going to kick me out! And then no one will be able to help me!*

I frantically pushed the dark power down. If it erupted and did something to anybody in the room, I had no doubt the community would never welcome me back again.

"Daria's here at my request." Wes's authoritative tone cut through the room. "As you can see, she has an extraordinary power. We're hoping to teach other witches to cultivate magic similar to what you witnessed tonight."

Priscilla snorted. "That was witch magic? I've never seen any witch do something like that. But that still doesn't explain why she went into that room. She should have been supervised." She gave a pointed look at Logan.

"I'm sorry." The apology gushed out of my lips like water from a fire hydrant. "I should have stayed where I was. Logan told me not to move. I didn't listen. Honestly, I'm so sorry that I harmed your friend."

Priscilla twirled toward me. "My friend? My *friend?*" she screeched. "He's not my friend! He's my brother! And you almost killed him!" Fury filled her words, and I again wished I could disappear right then and there.

"Enough." Wes held up a hand. "It's quite obvious that everybody's emotions are running high right now, and the more I hear about this, the more I see that it truly was an accident. A preventable accident—" Wes raised an eyebrow when Priscilla opened her mouth again. She snapped it closed then Wes addressed Logan. "You are not to leave her side again. Do you understand?"

Logan's jaw locked. "Yes, sir."

Wes clasped his hands behind his back and turned to Priscilla. "Last I heard, Phoenix was doing okay. He's expected to make a full recovery. Now, we're going to let Rose finish up so Daria can be discharged. I want everybody to turn in for the night. This matter is closed."

"Seriously?" The other woman in the group stepped forward. Short, spiky red hair covered her head, and the pointy tips of her ears gave away her species—fairy. "She almost killed Phoenix, and we're told she gets a free pass because of some freak magic she has? Don't you think a warning sign should be hung around her neck? So everyone can steer clear of the new freak?"

I stiffened, the blood draining from my face.

"Watch yourself, Chloe," Logan said in a calm but chilling voice.

"Or what, wolf? You'll sic the new freak on me?"

Fear and humiliation shot through me, and the dark power rolled violently. My breath came faster as I tried desperately to control it.

But before I could respond, Logan pushed away from the wall, advancing toward her. "Keep your fucking mouth shut, Chloe, and show her some respect."

"Or what?"

His jaw tightened, and veins in his neck strained. "Or…"

She took a step closer, her swagger cocky. "She's a freak, and you *know* it."

Logan's body shook, and the muscle in his jaw looked about to poke out of his skin. He shook his head, as if struggling with something.

"You must have it bad for this bitch—"

Out of nowhere, dominant energy shot from Logan and poured through the room.

I gasped.

His magic was so strong that my breath stopped, and my heart seized. The urge to run and hide filled me with adrenaline. I'd never felt anything like it. It flowed over my skin, prickling my nerves.

My dark power stirred violently, but I fought it. I didn't know what was worse. The coldness of my dark trying to erupt or the suffocating magic pouring from my boyfriend.

Nausea threatened to overwhelm me.

Logan's hands clenched into fists, and he gritted his teeth before the sound of clothes ripping filled the air. Then the air shimmered, and a huge black wolf stood where Logan had been. His tattered clothes littered the floor.

My eyes popped. My boyfriend had shifted so *fast*, faster than Jayden had been able to, even quicker than the one other time I'd seen Logan shift in Dillon Parker's mobile home.

In his wolf form, the dominant energy flowing from Logan increased a hundredfold, pouring off him in waves as his teeth bared, his hackles rose, and a deadly growl tore from his throat.

If I'd thought I'd wanted to hide before, I now wanted to bury myself alive. It didn't help that my control over my dark power was slipping. It fought violently inside me, wanting to rush to the surface.

*Fuck me and fuck all of this. Don't lose it, Daria!*

I clamped my jaw shut and fought the dark power violently. I pulled and clawed at it as it repeatedly tried to rise to the surface. It felt as if my muscles would explode from the exertion. Already, sweat dripped past my ear.

Logan's friends cowered behind him, while Chloe whimpered and stepped back, dipping her head. I continued to tremble under the covers while every other SF member crouched down, their shoulders folding inward.

Even Wes reacted.

Seeing that made my jaw drop. My dark power shot up at the opportunity. I snagged it at the last minute and pulled it down, but my surprise remained.

Logan was dominant enough that he caused the SF general to cower? Yet despite that, Logan willingly let Wes order him around for his job? What the hell did that mean?

A few more seconds passed, the power still emanating from Logan. Then, as quickly as he'd shifted to a wolf, he shifted back to human. Before I could blink, he was standing on two legs and wrapping a blanket that he'd snatched off a chair around his waist.

Some of the thick energy pulsing from him abated. I sucked in a breath, for the first time feeling that I could actually breathe as my dark power calmed.

"Fucking-A," one of the guys in Priscilla's group whispered.

The other four SF members of the separate squad all moved skittishly, keeping their gazes down but still giving Logan sharp, resentful looks when they dared to peek up.

When Logan finally dissipated whatever dominance

he'd unleashed, the fear on Chloe's face turned to fury.

She stepped closer to him. "You dare go alpha on our boss?" Chloe's gaze drifted to Wes. Given the veins protruding in Wes's neck, he was livid. "I wonder what Crystal will think about that."

My heart skipped when I heard another reference to the mystery woman just as Wes roared, "That's enough! All of you"—he pointed at the door—"out!"

Priscilla, Ray, Chloe, and the other two all glared at me when they stalked from the room.

Alexander, Brodie, and Jake gave me appeasing looks before they followed. Once the door closed behind them, I was left in the room with a terrified-looking Rose huddling in the corner, Wes, and Logan.

Wes stepped forward until he stood toe-to-toe with Logan. Barely controlled fury lined his face. "We'll speak tomorrow about what just happened here. My office, oh eight hundred hours. Right now, you're to take Daria back to your quarters and spend the night there. You are not to leave your residence. Is that understood, Major Smith?"

Logan's nostrils flared, but he still dipped his head, if a bit reluctantly. "Yes, sir."

Leaning closer to him, Wes said under his breath, "Don't make me regret giving you a chance in this role."

With that, the SF general spun on his heel and marched out of the room. Rose scurried after him, muttering something about getting me potions.

When it was just Logan and me in the room, he came to my side.

I swung my legs over the bed, but I let my gaze drift

to his muscled chest, unable to help myself. "What the hell was that?" A few goose bumps still peppered my skin.

His jaw tightened, his head dropping. "That was me losing control."

"So you're what? An alpha? Dominant over other werewolves? Over every other *species*? What just happened?"

Logan pulled my shoes out from under the bed and slipped them on my feet. The mundane domestic task was in complete contradiction to the absolute authority he'd just wielded over everyone, never mind that only a blanket covered his nakedness from the waist down. From his nonchalant attitude, his nakedness didn't perturb him at all, not even in a public place.

"Logan!" I said, my annoyance getting the better of me. "Answer me."

"Something like that," he finally replied.

From his quiet and reluctant tone, I knew he didn't want to talk about it, but I opened my mouth anyway. "So what is your role—"

"Here we are!" Rose breezed into the room, carrying two vials. A ruddy color filled her cheeks. She cast Logan a wary look, giving him a wide berth.

I swallowed the words on the tip of my tongue as Logan retreated to the corner. I stared at him, but he refused to make eye contact with me.

Rose handed me the two vials, forcing my attention to her. Her hands were shaking when she dropped the small bottles onto my palm. "Take these if you're in pain or need to sleep. One drop of the purple will give you a full night's rest without dreams, and one drop of the blue will ease your pain for an entire day. Apply them to your tongue and swallow."

I studied the liquid contents. The dark blue one was see-through liquid, and the other opaque violet one was thicker.

"Potions?" I asked, holding them up to the light. My nan had taught me how to make a few simple potions that any witch could manage, but like most of my magic that didn't involve healing, I rarely made them. My healing tours had completely taken over my life.

Rose's lips lifted in an overly bright smile. "Yes, that's correct. Two potions."

I shoved the potions into my pocket and eyed Logan, who was studying the ceiling as if it were the most fascinating piece of artwork.

Swallowing my irritation, I asked, "Is that a large part of your job here? To make healing potions for the sick?"

Rose nodded. "Of course. Only witches can heal." She winked, giving me a knowing smile.

She bustled to the corner and picked up my backpack and my purse, skittering away from Logan as quickly as she could. I'd completely forgotten about my things. Apparently, somebody had collected them for me after I'd left them by the elevator.

After helping me stand, she gave me my bags. Other than tired, I felt surprisingly fine.

"Just stop by or give us a call if anything doesn't feel right, but I have a sneaking suspicion you'll be as right as rain tomorrow." She eyed my leg. The white gauze still wound around my calf. "And I think you can take that off, dear. Whatever injury you had under there seems to be healed now."

With that, she turned and left the room, leaving me once again with an aloof werewolf who seemed intent on not answering my questions. But the last thing Rose said made me eye my lower leg. *The bite on my leg is already healed?*

Before I could check it, Jake, Alexander, and Brodie strode through the door. Jake chucked a bag of clothes at Logan.

Logan dipped his head in thanks before heading to the bathroom.

"You ready to get outta here?" Jake asked. He stepped forward and took my bags from me. A minute later, Logan emerged from the bathroom, once again fully dressed.

Alexander offered me his arm after pushing his glasses up his nose. "Can I help you walk?"

Following that, Brodie opened the door wide, gesturing for me go first.

Their attentiveness had me stammering, "I'm fine. Really, I am." I walked forward on my own, surprised at how good my leg felt, considering I'd been bitten by a werewolf only a day earlier and had survived a lethal hex only a few hours before.

I gave Logan another questioning look, but apparently, something on the bedspread was fascinating, because he seemed intent on studying it.

"You coming, bro?" Brodie asked Logan hesitantly.

The deeply brooding expression on Logan's face didn't waver. Not bothering to reply to Brodie, Logan strode through the door, leaving the rest of us to follow.

Frustration over my boyfriend's sudden distance rose in me. But as quickly as that came, so did a dose of curiosity. Just who exactly was Logan Smith?

# Chapter 13

Cool, nighttime wind caressed my cheeks when we stepped through the double doors of the healing center to the outside. Logan's friends seemed intent on not letting a moment of silence pass. If one wasn't asking me what I thought of the headquarters, then the others were relaying stories of missions they'd gone on and near-death experiences they'd dodged.

Some of their tales kept my attention, which I supposed was the entire reason they were telling them.

But every now and then, one of them would glance anxiously at Logan.

Logan still walked ahead of us, and he still refused to talk. His broad shoulders blocked my view of the barracks, and stiffness that hadn't been there earlier marred his gait. Even the beautiful night sky and the peaceful calm of the outdoors didn't lighten the mood.

"This is us," Brodie said a moment later, giving Logan another anxious side-eye.

We'd reached the barracks, and Brodie waved at the first door into the building. Similar to dorm buildings at colleges, the barracks looked like an apartment complex. They each stood three stories high and were dotted with windows, the brick exterior contrasting with the concrete buildings behind us.

Brodie reached for the door handle. "You two . . . uh . . . turning in for the night too?"

Logan nodded curtly.

I cocked my head. "So you're not going to the bars tonight, Brodie?"

Brodie raised a blond eyebrow. "That's where I'd be right now if you hadn't tried to kill somebody." As soon as he uttered the joke, he gave Logan another anxious look, but Logan's attention was focused on something in the distance, as if he wasn't even listening to us.

I offered a genuine smile. "Sorry to ruin your plans."

Brodie's shoulders relaxed a little before he winked. "Don't be. This was more exciting, anyway." He dipped his head before he turned and strolled inside.

"Goodnight, Daria. See you tomorrow." Jake handed over my bags, which he'd insisted on carrying the entire way, before giving Logan a wide berth.

Alexander pushed his glasses up his nose but also kept a few feet of distance between himself and my boyfriend. "Night."

After the three of them disappeared, Logan finally

waved to the other end of the barracks, coming out of whatever trance he'd been in. "I live down there."

"You don't live with those three?"

He shook his head. "Dominant wolves get their own living space."

*Why am I not surprised?*

We resumed walking, and the silence stretched between us. All that did was remind me that I was still getting to know Logan. He'd never mentioned before that he was dominant over his friends, and I still didn't really know who Crystal was, other than someone from back home.

I frowned. Although, it seemed pretty obvious Crystal was his ex—an ex who still had it bad for him. Since everyone kept mentioning her, I wondered if their breakup was fresh, or if they'd been really serious at one point. And given the text I saw from her the previous month—the text in which she'd stated that she missed him and wondered when he could call—I had a feeling she wanted to get back together with him.

Jealousy shot through me, making the dark power roll.

I took a deep breath and stuffed my hands into my pockets. It was possible I was right, that Crystal and Logan had been together for years and had only recently broken up. Or maybe Crystal was some kind of celebrity in the werewolf world, so their breakup had been public knowledge. Or maybe Crystal was another SF member who just happened to know Logan from their home state, and *that* was the reason everyone kept referring to her. Perhaps I'd seen Crystal during my SF tour, but since I'd had no idea what she looked like, I hadn't known.

That thought made me stumble.

Logan automatically reached for me, but I righted myself at the last moment, pulling away from him before he could touch me. Just thinking of Logan with another woman made the dark power angry.

*Very* angry.

I took several deep breaths, trying to push it down. The cold darkness hovered dangerously close to my fingertips.

Knowing the tension strumming through me wasn't going to diminish, and the only chance I had of calming the dark power was to know the full truth, I blurted, "Logan, who's Crystal? You gotta tell me. Who is she?"

His jaw tightened, but he wouldn't look at me.

I held my breath.

He kept walking, his footsteps quiet and his head down. The last door to the barracks waited ahead. I figured that was where we were headed.

"Logan?"

"I told you. She's a girl from back home and nobody you need to be worried about."

I groaned, the dark power growing again. He'd just given me the same damned evasive answer as he had the other week. "But *who* is she? An ex-girlfriend? Someone you had a fling with? Someone who works with you here? *Who?*" The urge to stomp my foot grew so strong that I had to take another deep breath.

The muscle in Logan's jaw ticked. For a moment, I didn't think he was going to answer, but then he said, "Just someone from back home. Okay?"

*In other words, he's not going to tell me.*

I closed my eyes and took a deep calming breath before opening them. Images of a young Logan laughing and running through Wyoming fields with a beautiful girl at his side flashed through my mind. Just the thought of someone who shared that history with him made me want to barf.

The door loomed in front of us. "This is me." He stopped at the door, his expression apprehensive, but his stubborn resolve told me he wasn't going to divulge his past with Crystal—no matter how many times I asked.

The dark tension and brooding jealousy coursing through me felt like bugs crawling under my skin, but at that moment, I knew what I needed to do.

More than anything, I wanted the carefree, easygoing laughter that had filled our time together from before Logan revealed his dominance and before Crystal's ghost slunk between us.

I didn't want this, and I didn't want his past to come between us. After all, whoever Crystal was, she was in the *past*. I needed to remember that.

*No more questions about Crystal, Dar, just stop.*

Besides, whatever the truth was—as much as morbid curiosity urged me to learn it—I didn't actually want to know. In fact, it was probably better if I didn't, and perhaps Logan realized that.

Forcing myself to take another deep breath, I opened the door and stepped into the building. It took another moment to calm the dark power, but when I finally felt in control, I peeked up at Logan. "Are you doing okay, by the way?"

His head snapped back, as if surprised by my question. "I'm fine."

"Anyone can see you're not fine."

It suddenly occurred to me that for the first time since I'd met him, Logan was upset about something that had nothing to do with me, and all I'd cared about was some girl from his past. I hadn't cared about him in the *present.*

*Worst girlfriend ever.*

I mentally kicked myself.

The door closed behind us, but he remained silent.

"You don't seem fine. You seem upset," I added.

He ran a hand through his hair.

"You can talk to me, too, you know. It's not a one-way street. You're always caring for me, looking after me, but I can do the same for you."

His eyes glowed subtly, a tenderness that hadn't been there a moment ago shining through. "You're incredible. Do you know that?"

A small smile lifted my lips, the dark power calming completely at the shift in energy between us. "If I didn't know better, I'd say you were avoiding the subject."

That groove appeared between his eyes again. "I'm not used to talking about myself. My job isn't to worry about me. It's to worry about others."

"You mean as an . . . alpha or whatever?"

His jaw locked, and I held my breath.

Then, he nodded.

I let out the breath I'd been holding. "And since I'm now asking about you, that doesn't sit well with you?"

"No, it's not that." He raised a finger and brushed it

across my cheek, the movement quick and fleeting. Still, it was enough touch for my dark power to tingle, but that was all. My light stayed calmed with him, and a contented sigh ran through me. "I'm just not used to it."

I stepped closer to him. "I want to be here for you too. To be honest, I'm not entirely sure what's going on with you right now, but I want to understand."

His gaze held mine, the glow in his eyes intensifying. "I lost my shit back there," he finally replied. "I'm not very happy with myself right now."

"Does that happen often? That you lose control?"

"No. I can't remember the last time I did." A dark look crossed his face again. "Speaking like that to my friends, my fellow SF members, and my boss . . . commanding everyone like that . . . commanding *you* like that." He shook his head, his lip curling. "That's not to be taken lightly, and I shouldn't have done it."

The memory of goose bumps rising along my skin and wanting to cower under the covers flashed to the forefront of my mind. "No, I suppose it's not, but you have to admit, Chloe was really goading you. She kept pushing you for a reaction."

He scowled. "And I gave her one."

"You were standing up for me," I said hesitantly. "You were protecting me. I'm not saying that forgives all behaviors on your part, but your actions originated from a good place, and I . . ." I bit my lip. "It means a lot to me when you have my back."

He chuckled softly. "I should blame you for this, is that it?" His amusement vanished. "You bring out something in me, Daria Gresham. A side of myself I can't control."

I wanted so much to step forward and touch him. "You bring out feelings in me too. Things I've never felt before and can't control either."

The light in his eyes grew, but he abruptly looked away and raked a hand through his hair. "Still. I can't be doing shit like that. I could get kicked out of the SF." That groove appeared between his eyes again, reminding me of his meeting with Wes in the morning.

"Yeah, I get it. You wield a power I didn't even know you had, but right now, maybe you should cut yourself some slack."

He smiled. "Is that your official recommendation?"

"It is. And *trust me*, I'm a healer." I waggled my eyebrows.

He laughed, the sound sending an eruption of fresh shivers along my skin. The shift in his mood and the stormy look in his eyes fading made lightness that hadn't been there in a while fill my chest.

"So," I said coyly, "are you going to show me where you live?"

His smile stayed in place, the agitated energy coming off him disappearing. "Follow me."

# Chapter 14

Logan led me down the hall. At the last door, he stopped and inserted a key into a lock. Just above the dead bolt hovered a holographic panel.

"What's that?" I asked, pointing at it.

"That's what I use if I forget my keys. It can unlock the door without a key . . . another invention the sorcerers came up with." He swung open the door. "Brodie uses them a lot, especially when he's been out drinking for the night and loses his keys."

We stepped into Logan's apartment, and he closed the door behind us before moving into the living room to turn on a lamp.

Soft light flooded the room, and I kicked off my shoes, my feet sinking into thick carpet. I paused, taking it all in.

Off to the right lay a large living room with two couches, a few tables, a standing lamp, and a TV hanging on the wall.

On the left, a counter with stools that overlooked the open kitchen cut an L shape in the room. The kitchen wasn't big, but it held all of the necessities. For the most part, it looked like a normal kitchen devoid of any magical devices.

His entire apartment felt masculine. It didn't have any knickknacks or pictures on the walls. The entire color scheme was silver and dark blue, a slightly modern feeling due to the simplicity, but I liked it.

"My bedroom's back that way." He nodded toward the hallway off the living room. "Just across from it is the bathroom." He took my bags and set them on the floor. "How are you feeling? Did you want to sit down? Take a shower? Watch TV?"

I glanced at my leg. Even though I felt tired and hungry, Rose had been right. My werewolf bite no longer plagued me, and I was curious to see what waited under the bandage. "Yeah, a shower sounds good."

He led me to the bathroom and pulled out a fresh towel. Logan's scent and broad shoulders filled the cramped space. Tingles of awareness shot through me. One step to the right, one lift of my hand, and I would be running my palm along his back, feeling his hard torso and sinewy muscles.

Logan turned, his nostrils flaring and his eyes hooded. "Too bad I can't shower with you."

My breath stopped as I pictured Logan—*naked*—in

the shower with me, running his large hands over my body, cupping my breasts, sucking my core.

"Yeah," I replied breathlessly. "Too bad."

With a regretful look in his eyes, he stepped out, closing the door behind him. Alone in the room, I stripped my clothes off and pulled the gauze from my leg.

All thoughts of Logan's hands running along my skin vanished. My jaw dropped. *No way!*

I turned my leg back and forth, examining my smooth calf. The puncture holes from the werewolf bite were *completely* gone.

I closed my eyes, tuning in to the dark power. It rushed forward, filling my belly with coldness. It felt so different from my light.

My eyes flashed open again, going to my nonexistent wound. Not even a faint scar remained. *The dark power did this.*

I didn't know how I knew that, but I did. My light couldn't heal me, not unless I was in a healing session and burning away somebody else's disease. That meant the darkness had to be behind it.

Trembling, I turned on the shower and stepped under the warm spray, then I scrubbed myself clean.

I concentrated on the various products Logan had in his shower, anything to distract myself from my latest discovery.

Men's shaving cream, a razor, and shampoo that held a hint of sandalwood sat on the shelf. The sparse products matched the rest of his apartment's simplistic design.

Once clean, I hastily turned off the water and stepped

out, grabbing the towel hanging on the rack. When I turned to grab my bag, my naked body stared back at me in the large mirror hanging over the sink.

I trailed a hand down my bare chest, over the heavy weight of my breasts, to my stomach. Just beneath my palm, my powers responded, my light rattling in the cage that I kept it in. I closed my eyes. In a way, my light and the dark power were like life forces inside me, like unborn twins I would never give birth to.

"Dar?" A soft knock came on the door.

I jumped.

"I heard the shower stop. Are you hungry?"

I hastily wrapped the towel around myself. "Yeah, I'm actually starving. I'll be right out!" I dug around in my bag for my pajamas.

As usual, my pajamas weren't matronly. I donned the short shorts and the thin top before running a comb through my hair. Once done, I eyed myself again in the mirror. Dark circles through my shirt hinted at my areolas. A flush stained my cheeks.

*He's going to think you're doing this on purpose.*

When I opened the door, Logan still stood in the hallway, and his gaze immediately dipped down.

My nipples hardened, and a rush of desire clenched my core.

His jaw locked, the muscle ticking in the corner. "Fuck me," he whispered and hastily took a step away. "Be right back."

He disappeared from the hallway, moving so fast that I knew his werewolf gene had kicked in. A second later, he reappeared, holding one of his sweatshirts out. "You'd better put this on and zipper it completely closed. For my sake. Please."

The desire in my core flamed. "Not just for your sake." I zippered his sweatshirt to my throat, and the material effectively covered me to midthigh in a huge shapeless tent.

He turned stiffly, and I followed him back to the kitchen, trying desperately to not devour his sexy swagger. *Down, girls.*

My nose twitched, catching heavenly scents coming from the stove. I took another deep breath, trying to douse my desire by focusing on dinner.

"You know how to cook?" I settled onto a stool at the counter, overlooking the kitchen.

Logan went to the stove and stirred something in a pot. "A little. I'm not a chef, but I keep myself from starving."

From the scent coming from the bubbling sauce, I guessed he'd made something Italian. Sure enough, Logan grabbed a box of pasta and dumped the noodles into a pot of boiling water.

With his back to me, I let my gaze wander over his broad shoulders and heavily muscled back. His muscles bunched and tensed with his movements. When he turned to the pantry to grab some garlic, my gaze dipped to his flat abdomen and the subtle swagger of his hips.

Swallowing tightly, I pulled his sweatshirt more tightly around me, just as he turned a knowing look my way, his nostrils flaring.

A few minutes later, he served up two plates of steaming spaghetti covered in a rich meat sauce.

"Wow, this smells good." My stomach grumbled, reminding me it had been a long time since lunch.

"Wine?" he asked, holding up a bottle of Merlot.

"Sure."

After sitting on the stool beside me, he held up his drink. "Cheers. To our first dinner alone together."

I cocked my head. "What about that fast food restaurant we went to?" That had been after I'd met Dillon Parker at the diner, before I knew he was my stalker.

"We weren't alone. That was in public."

I clinked my glass with his. "In that case, cheers. Hopefully, this is the first of many."

The ring around his irises grew brighter, but so did an emotion in his eyes. *Worry?* But he turned away before I could fully assess his reaction to my toast.

I took a sip of the wine, my hand trembling. Dry berry flavors burst over my tongue, but I barely tasted it.

Logan's worry only reminded me of my current reality.

I had a dark power that could kill people and I couldn't control it, yet a voice in my mind had told me how to fight the rogues which made no sense whatsoever.

My body recognized Logan as a potential mate, but if I stayed with him and he became the father of my sole child, I had no idea if my attraction to him would remain. Because even though I genuinely *liked* Logan, my out-of-control lust for him could all be linked to him being a potential mate. Who was to say that attraction would stay once he fathered my child? It certainly hadn't for my mother and my nan.

And the only potential hope I had at finding answers to explain anything were in the community, but already, I'd made enemies, and I'd only just arrived.

I sipped my wine again and did my best to concentrate on our first dinner together.

# Chapter 15

I twirled spaghetti onto my fork and popped the bite into my mouth. The rich sauce and the soft noodles distracted me momentarily. I closed my eyes and savored it. "This is really good."

"I'll tell my mom that. It's her favorite meal."

I was in the midst of twirling pasta on my fork, but my movements paused, my breath quickening. There it was, the perfect opportunity to learn more about him and his family.

I cleared my throat and resumed twirling. "How . . . uh, how often do you see your mom?"

Logan took another large bite, his jaw working rhythmically. "I used to go home every few weeks. Now, not so much."

*Okaaaay* . . . I made myself take a bite and chew so my eagerness wouldn't be so apparent. "What's your home like?"

"We own a ranch in the mountains. Dad has around two thousand head of cattle, and every time I'm home, I help him with work. Since my brother still lives in my hometown and since my sister still lives at home, they're always there, too, and so is my mom."

"Is your entire family werewolves?"

"Yeah, but only Dad and my brother can turn into wolves, but Mom and my sister are carriers of the gene."

"That's right. Cause only men can be werewolves." I took another sip of wine. "Does that mean your mom and sister are fully human even if they're carriers?"

"No. As carriers, they're not fully human since they have heightened senses and strength. They just don't turn into wolves."

"Huh." I tried to imagine growing up as Logan had, in one spot with my family surrounding me, no a *pack* surrounding me. I couldn't. Logan's life and mine were complete opposites. "Is there a large werewolf community in Wyoming?"

He nodded. "Most of Montana, Idaho, and Wyoming are home to werewolves. There are only three packs in the country, and we tend to stick pretty close together, even though we don't always get along."

Three packs. Okay, I hadn't known that. Finally, I was getting somewhere. "So, the wolves in your pack all, like, live in the same town or something?"

"No. We're scattered in towns throughout the state, but we own the town where the majority of the pack resides."

"You *own* the town?"

"More or less. We own all of the land, and the only residents are pack members."

"How big is it?"

He cocked his head. "At last count, around ten thousand members."

"And humans in the surrounding towns don't suspect anything unusual about your werewolf town?"

"Not really. The nearest towns are about fifty miles away. They know us as being a tight-knit, unfriendly community that doesn't appreciate outsiders. We've had humans try to buy land and want to join us, but we refuse. Cause if they can't buy land and houses are never for sale, it's kinda hard to move in. For the most part, they leave us alone since we don't cause any problems. It helps that we're good neighbors, even if we're unfriendly."

I swirled the wine in my glass, taking another sip before trying to ask casually, "And what role does your dad play in your pack?"

Logan dipped his head and forked another bite of spaghetti. "He's . . . uh . . . the alpha."

*Surprise, surprise.* "So that means he's in charge of the entire pack?"

"More or less."

I took another sip of wine. "Is that why you're dominant over your friends? Because your dad is dominant?"

"You could say that."

I frowned since his evasiveness was returning after

telling me so much. "Does that mean you'll be alpha one day? Because you're dominant too?"

He grabbed his wine and took another drink before setting it down. "That's the plan."

His tone indicated that he wasn't happy about it. I remembered Wes's words. *Don't make me regret giving you a chance in this role.*

I twirled another forkful of spaghetti and squirmed. Logan's body language was growing more closed off by the second, but I desperately wanted to know more.

"So . . . you don't want to be alpha?"

His jaw tightened, but he didn't reply.

When he refused to answer, I decided to keep pushing, even if it meant pulling teeth. "Why don't you?"

Several seconds passed. It was long enough I thought he *wouldn't* reply, when he said quietly, "Certain expectations come from being alpha, which means we don't always have a choice about certain aspects of our lives. I don't like that."

*Choice? Choice about what?* But that shutting-down expression veiled his face again, growing sharper by the second. I backpedaled, switching subjects to keep him talking.

"So how do things work in the werewolf world? Is the alpha the president or something?"

His lips quirked up. "President? Um, no, but he is in charge, and he is responsible for the well-being of the pack."

"That sounds like a lot of responsibility."

He moved his fork around his plate. "It is."

"Can you tell me more about what it's like to be a

werewolf? Could you shift from the very beginning? You know, like when you were a baby?"

He laughed. "No, babies don't shift. The gene doesn't activate until puberty. The first time I shifted, I was thirteen."

"What was it like?"

He twirled another bite of spaghetti onto his fork. "Weird. Exhilarating. Powerful feeling. I knew it was coming. My parents had prepared me for it, but to actually *feel* the magic activate and to *feel* my wolf coming through and becoming a part of me . . . I don't even know how to describe it."

Since I'd switched the conversation to safer ground, that haunted look had left his eyes. He opened up again, telling me all sorts of things I didn't know.

Apparently, everything worked off a hierarchy in the werewolf world, the more dominant families had the power and control, and the less dominant families filled the roles that were considered less desirable. Since his dad was alpha, I knew his family had to be the most dominant.

"So can a werewolf only come from a male and female werewolf?" I finished off my wine, my head spinning a bit from the alcohol.

"No. A full-blooded werewolf can sire a werewolf child with a human or another supernatural, but the gene doesn't always manifest. There's a fifty-fifty chance the child won't be a werewolf if the other parent is human or another supernatural."

"And if their child is a girl?"

"The same rules apply. Any female born werewolf

won't ever turn into a wolf, but if she's a hybrid, she has a fifty percent chance of carrying the gene and showing werewolf characteristics herself."

"Those characteristics being heightened senses and strength?" After Logan nodded, I added, "But a child between a male and female werewolf *always* produces a werewolf child?"

"Correct."

"That's surprising then, that there aren't any humans in your pack if there's a chance they can still produce a werewolf child."

"There can't be humans in our pack, and that has nothing to do with breeding. Remember what I told you before about how the SF laws changed ten years ago? Supernaturals can't reveal themselves to human partners anymore."

"Oh, that's right. I forgot. So is that why there aren't any humans in your pack?"

"The law is part of the reason, but it's also because we tend to breed within our pack and surrounding packs. You have to understand, dominance rules *everything* in the werewolf world. Even though females never change into werewolves, they still carry the gene and can pass on dominance to their children." He popped another forkful of spaghetti into his mouth and swallowed. He was on his second plate. "Some say offspring of two dominant werewolf parents makes for stronger wolf offspring, therefore the chance of having a more dominant son increases."

"Can less dominant wolves still have a dominant son? Is that even possible?"

"It's possible just not as likely. While shifts in power don't often occur, the possibility still remains. That's the main reason the werewolf community tends to breed within itself. Each family hopes to birth the next generation of super-dominants, which ultimately results in a different family rising to the top."

"Wow. That sounds intense."

"It can be. Dynamics can be weird among families, especially when sons are coming of age. Parents practically hold their breaths to see what dominance level manifests in their kids."

"And you're pretty dominant, right? Considering what happened in the recovery room?" I was almost loath to bring it up, but so far, Logan had remained talking, and I wanted to soak up every bit of information I could about him and his family while I had the chance.

"Yeah." His tone almost sounded bitter.

"Is that weird? Since Wes is always ordering you around?"

He shifted on his stool. I knew I'd just hit another sore spot.

"Kind of," he finally replied. "A lot of times, I have to fight my nature, but it's good for learning self-control."

Steering our conversation away from what seemed to be another sensitive topic, I asked, "So is your joining the SF something all werewolves do?"

His hand stilled, his wine halfway to his lips.

*Or maybe I just hit another nerve . . .* I forked another bite, pretending to not notice his sudden reluctance.

"No, it's not something all werewolves do. I'm the first in my family to join the SF."

I swallowed the mouthful I'd been chewing uneasily. From his tone, I'd *definitely* hit rocky territory again.

"Why did you join?"

He shrugged, pushing food around his plate. "I wanted to try something new and get away from . . ." His fork moved faster, squishing the remains of food. "I don't know. I guess I wanted to avoid some of my responsibilities back home."

He didn't elaborate.

I set my utensils down, no longer hungry for the few remaining bites of pasta that had grown cold. I could have been wrong, but it seemed I'd hit the core of Logan's caginess about his life back in Wyoming.

Swallowing the uneasiness in my throat, I asked something I'd been wondering about our entire dinner, because from what I'd learned so far, Logan was a big deal in the werewolf world, a *very* big deal, yet he'd tried to hide that and blend in with the masses.

But try as he might, I knew there was no running from a family legacy. Of all people, I knew that too well.

"And your family won't mind that I'm not a werewolf?" I asked quietly.

Logan set his fork down and pushed his food away then picked up his wine and drained the rest of it in one gulp. "You'll encounter a lot of different opinions in the werewolf community. It's best to just ignore them."

*That doesn't sound reassuring at all.*

"Do you want dessert?" He stood and cleared our plates. A loud clatter made me jump when he dumped the dishes in the sink.

"Uh, no. I'm fine. I'm pretty full, actually."

He turned on the water, the loud sound of the spray filling the kitchen. Normally, I would have slid off my stool to help, but considering that Logan was scrubbing the dishes so hard he was practically attacking them, I figured letting him work out his aggression alone was probably better.

I cleared my throat and switched subjects completely. "So do all fairies look like Chloe and Millie?"

Logan glanced over his shoulder and some of the tense lines around his mouth relaxed. "When they're not wearing their glamour, yeah, the pointy ears, glowing skin, brightly colored hair, and razor-sharp teeth are how all fairies look."

"So what do they look like when they're wearing glamour?"

"Like you or me. They're very good at blending in with the public. You could walk by a fairy on the street and not even know it, even though you're a supernatural."

I raised my eyebrows and took another sip of wine. "You're saying I could've met fairies at some point in my life and not known it?"

"You most likely have."

I shook my head, once again amazed that the entire supernatural community had been right beneath my nose my entire life. "Millie seemed pretty friendly. I wouldn't mind seeing her again, but Chloe, on the other hand . . ." I raised my eyebrows.

"That's just because you hurt Phoenix. Try not to take it personally. She's not exactly the warm and friendly type, and her hostility tonight is kinda her norm, but I'm guessing she went after you because of their recent assignment. They just got back from Africa and had some close calls while they were there. They're lucky they all made it back, which has made all of them a bit high-strung lately."

"Are your jobs really that dangerous?"

"Sometimes." His voice dropped, and with a crashing realization, I remembered something Logan had said to me weeks before, on a hill overlooking a rest stop, back when he was my bodyguard and long before I knew of the supernatural community or that he was a werewolf.

He'd had friends die—two, if I recalled correctly.

*"It was years ago, but it's something I'll carry with me until I die."*

But despite watching his friends die in what I assumed was an SF mission, Logan still preferred the SF versus facing his responsibilities at home. That in itself said everything about what he was avoiding.

"What were they doing in Africa?" I asked.

"Tracking down a ninki nanka. One had strayed from its swamp and was terrorizing a village. We don't have to deal with them very often, but every twenty years or so, a team is dispatched to deal with one. It's only when they leave the swamp that problems happen."

"A ninki nanka?"

"A supernatural African beast. That particular one is rather nasty. Dangerous too."

"Is that why you're so close with Brodie, Alexander, and Jake? Because the four of you have been in situations where you might have been killed?"

"That's part of it. We also grew up together. We're from the same pack, and I've known them my entire life."

"So you all joined the SF together?"

"Yes."

From his clipped response, I knew he didn't want to delve back into werewolf talk. The loud faucet spray finally stopped after he rinsed all the dishes and loaded the dishwasher. Following that, he topped off our glasses with the last of the wine.

I hastily took a drink, needing the soothing effects of alcohol more than ever.

"How's your leg doing?" he asked, sitting beside me once again.

My lips parted. I'd completely forgotten to tell him about my healed wound. "It's fine. In fact, I'm completely healed."

His eyebrows knit together when I showed him my calf. "Amazing. You healed as fast as a werewolf."

I didn't tell him that I normally didn't heal that fast and that the only explanation was that the dark power healed me.

If anything, the event in the training room only solidified how incredibly powerful it was. Not only could the dark power kill somebody at a moment's notice, but it could protect me as well. And while a part of that was comforting, it was also terrifying. Whatever now lived inside me had grown incredibly strong. I could feel it. It was like the more I used it, the more it thrived.

The bottom line—I needed to learn how to control it or get rid of it, because if I couldn't control it, I would inevitably kill someone again.

Not wanting to dwell on the dark power, I said, "Did you know my entire life I thought nobody else who could supernaturally heal existed? And all along there was an entire coven of witches that could heal, too, living here at headquarters. I bet my mom and my nan would have loved to meet them."

Logan's eyebrows rose in an incredulous expression. "You think the witches here can heal like you do?"

"Can't they? Back at the healing center, Rose did something to me with her magic. I felt it. I was getting worked up and anxious right after I woke up, and she stopped it by fluttering her fingers over me and casting a spell."

"It's true that some witches possess healing magic, but they can't do anything like what you can." He shook his head. "I don't know any witch alive who can bring somebody back from the brink of death, or heal paralysis, or find someone's cancer and eradicate it, or banish mental illness." He paused, twirling his wine glass between his fingers. "You really don't know how special you are, do you?"

"So . . . my family *is* different? We're not like the other witches here?"

"No. You're nothing like them. The entire community knows that your family's history and abilities are unique—that's why you're famous. The other witches, they all have their own types of powers, but the healing witches don't hold a candle to you. What you experienced from Rose tonight, with her lessening your anxiety, is about the extent of what a healing witch can do. Their potions are pretty handy, though, especially if you're suffering from a nasty wound that takes longer than most to heal."

"Oh." I didn't know what else to say. All night, I'd assumed I'd finally met other witches like me, but according to Logan, no witch was like me. I drained the rest of my wine, my head swimming more.

Logan collected our glasses. "You ready to turn in? Eight o'clock will be here before we know it, and considering what happened earlier, I'd better not be late."

According to the clock on the stove, it was almost midnight.

I sat up straighter while Logan started the dishwasher. "What's the plan for tomorrow?"

"After I meet with Wes, we'll see the scholars. He was able to reserve two from the courts."

I still had no idea what he was referring to when he spoke about the scholars and the courts, but a loud yawn stopped my curiosity. It had been a long day, and the wine was aiding my sleepiness.

"Do you really think the scholars will be able to help me?"

He placed his hands on his hips. His strong chest muscles pressed against his T-shirt. "If anybody is going to have answers and will help figure out what's happened to you, it's them."

# Chapter 16

Ten minutes later, Logan and I stood in his bedroom listening to the hum of the dishwasher as it carried into the room.

A navy-blue coverlet spread across his massive king-sized bed which took up most of the room. The blue contrasted nicely with the steel bed frame. Similar to the rest of his home, simple and sparse furnishings with clean lines and no flair filled the space.

I toyed with the zipper on the sweatshirt as I contemplated our sleeping arrangements.

Logan reached for a pillow and the spare blanket at the end of the bed. "You take the bed. I'll sleep on the floor."

"No!" I jumped, dropping the zipper. "This is your

house. I'll take the floor. You take the bed."

He glowered down at me and took a step closer, the pillow and the blanket forgotten. He stood only a hair's breadth away, just far enough so that we weren't touching but close enough that I could *feel* him. Warmth radiated from his body, and if I closed my eyes and inhaled, I would be flooded with his scent.

"You're taking the bed, Dar. Don't even try to argue. There's no way I'm going to sleep up there while you're on the floor."

"But I—"

"No."

I ran my hand along the bed. "This is a pretty big bed. Maybe if we put pillows between us, we wouldn't have to worry about me touching you."

Even though my stomach lurched at the thought of accidentally hurting Logan during the night, I also didn't want him sleeping on the hard floor.

"I appreciate the thought, but it's not happening. Get in the bed."

I sighed loudly. His insistence that I take the more comfortable spot reminded me of who Logan was. He always put my needs first. Always. Whether that could be explained by his alpha side shining through or it simply being who he was, I didn't know, but when he'd been my bodyguard, he hadn't given his well-being a second thought. He'd always thought about my safety and comfort before his.

I opened my mouth to argue again, telling myself that for once he was going to put himself first, but Logan beat me to it.

"Dar, I'm not sleeping on the bed. Just get under the damn covers so you don't freeze to death standing there."

A chill had already settled in the room. Summertime's end neared. If the cool breeze trickling in through the cracked window held any indication, it was going to be a cold night.

"Fine." I sighed in exasperation and slipped off the sweatshirt.

My breasts strained against my thin nightshirt, my nipples immediately hardening in the cool air. Logan's entire body tensed, his gaze dipping down. I snatched the covers back on the bed, dove under the sheets, and pulled them to my chin before my boobs could make another embarrassing display.

A relieved sigh escaped Logan when my entire body was covered by the thick blanket.

Following that, he took three long strides to the far wall, dropped the spare pillow on the floor beneath the windowsill, and then rolled his blanket out.

I watched as he arranged his bed. With his back to me, he raised his shirt over his head. My eyes widened and my breath caught when his smooth tanned skin appeared.

His muscles rippled when he tossed his shirt in the corner. Next came his jeans. He slid them off and kicked them aside, revealing strong legs peppered with dark hair. Clad in only his boxers, he dropped to the ground and pulled the blanket over him, his head settling with a thump on the pillow.

"Night, babe."

I hastily reached over and turned off the lamp.

Moonlight flooded the room, the round orb hanging just above the horizon.

My gaze darted to the dark ceiling, my breath shallow. Once again, my hormones shot into overdrive as images of Logan's body flooded my mind.

Tingling started deep in my belly, next to my powers. I closed my eyes tightly and tried to stop the unbidden images that kept bombarding my mind—images of Logan sliding under the covers next to me, his hand running lightly up my thigh, his warm mouth pressing kisses against my neck, then his tongue doing delicious things to my ear. My heart beat frantically as I squirmed on the mattress.

A growl came abruptly from where Logan lay. "If you want me to sleep at all tonight, Dar, you're gonna have to stop it."

"Stop what?" I squeaked.

Rustling sounded from where he lay. "You're giving off pheromones like a bitch in heat. I can smell your sex. I can smell that you're ready for me. It's hard enough not being able to touch you, but knowing how badly you want me . . ." More rustling. "I might have to sleep on the couch."

Hearing that Logan could sense the sweet ache between my thighs made me clench my legs together more. But that only heightened the tingles. I sighed heavily, my voice coming out in a whisper, "I can't help it. It's what you do to me."

"Dar . . ."

"It's true. I'm sorry. I'll try to . . . I don't know." My hand slid between my thighs. My sex ached. Just the feel of my fingers brushing against it caused a moan low in my throat.

Before I could clamp a hand over my mouth, Logan was on the bed next to me. He did it so quickly, like he'd flown across the room and landed on the mattress.

I snatched my hand away from my sex and looked at him with wide eyes. "Logan! What are you doing up here? You can't touch me. You know that. I could kill you!"

Desire filled his eyes, making them glow gold. Ragged breaths lifted his chest. His mouth tightened. "I know I said I wouldn't touch you. I know that I promised that. But fuck, Dar, this is harder than I thought it would be." He closed his eyes and inhaled. "You have no idea what scent you're giving off. Every werewolf within a mile can probably smell your sex." A low growl sounded in his throat again. "And the thought of another male smelling that makes me fucking crazy. Fuck, I want to claim you." He took a deep breath and opened his eyes.

"What's this claiming thing you keep talking about?" My fingers strayed lower again, as if on their own accord. The ache between my thighs had grown exponentially.

A muscle ticked in his jaw. "Are you touching yourself again?"

I dipped my chin. "Maybe."

His jaw worked faster. "Claiming is a werewolf thing. Males will mark a female as theirs, then other wolves know she's off limits."

"And you want to claim me now?"

"More than I've ever wanted anything in my life, but I'd have to touch you to do it."

Just hearing how much he wanted me did things to

me I'd never experienced.

His nostrils flared again, his eyes glowing brighter. "Make yourself cum. Maybe if you have release, you'll stop giving off these scents, and I'll be able to control myself better. It's taking everything in me right now to not bury my cock in you."

"Make myself cum?" I squeaked. *In front of him?*

He slowly pulled back the covers from me, the cotton sheet sliding along my skin. Just the feel of the softness trailing over my limbs while his heavy gaze avidly devoured my breasts and my stomach as they emerged made my sex swell even more.

He closed his eyes and inhaled deeply. "Touch yourself, Dar," he said hoarsely. "Touch yourself until you orgasm."

His gaze was bright when his eyes opened, his breathing coming in short pants. My eyes locked with his as my fingers strayed lower. "I don't usually touch myself."

"Do it for me."

I broke eye contact long enough to let my gaze trail down his hard chest to his crotch. In the moonlight, his boxers tented out, hinting at the huge erection beneath them.

Seeing that made me squirm again. I settled my fingers on my core and began rubbing myself. My body responded instantly, arching off the bed, a moan filling the back of my throat. Logan was right. I was like a bitch in heat.

"That's it, babe. Keep rubbing yourself."

I locked gazes with him again. His breathing grew

more and more ragged as my fingers dipped and played. I pushed my pajama shorts aside, cool air washing against my swollen lips.

His pupils dilated when he saw my sex in the moonlight. "Fuck, Dar. You're as beautiful as I imagined you'd be." His large hand strayed to the edge of his boxers. He inched it down, and his erection sprang free.

I gasped, the swell of my sex growing a hundredfold.

His hand wrapped around his hard length, and he began to pump it up and down. "God, you're so wet. I can smell it from here."

When I saw him touch himself, my fingers moved faster, making my breath catch in my throat.

He inched closer, kneeling lower on the bed but still being careful not to touch me. "I just want to smell you. I need to smell you."

The mattress dipped when he leaned down and brought his face closer to my sex. Even though air still separated us, I'd never felt more aroused in my life. His large hand was still wrapped around his erection as he moved his face closer to my core.

My fingers moved faster, the need within me rising higher.

"I want to lick you so bad right now." He sucked in a breath and blew softly on my sex.

I moaned as the pressure built inside me.

"That's it, babe. I can smell that you're getting close. Cum for me."

I rubbed harder, the pressure building higher and higher. I opened my eyes just long enough to see Logan's entire body tense as he sat back on his haunches. His large hand pumped his erection faster.

Seeing that sent me over the edge. I shouted my release as wave after wave of pleasure shot through me. Logan's shout came next, and I opened my eyes just as his seed pumped all over his hand.

I tried not to stare, but when he hung his head back with his mouth open as his strong hand stroked his rigid length, I couldn't take my eyes away. I was still a virgin, and the realm of sex was still so new to me. I greedily watched as his dick grew soft, his shoulders relaxing while a heady glaze coated his eyes.

He collapsed on the bed beside me then grabbed a tissue to wipe his hand. As he propped himself up on his elbow, a lazy smile stretched across his face.

A few moments of silence passed, both of us panting heavily.

"Even though I'd prefer to actually touch you, damn, woman. That was good."

My cheeks heated. "It was?"

He nodded, his eyelids hooded. "There's something about you, Daria Gresham. No woman has ever aroused me so much."

I tried to bite back my smile but couldn't. "Really? Do you mean that?"

His voice turned husky. "Yeah, I mean that, and when I smelled you tonight and you started touching yourself—"

"I've never . . . I mean, what I just did, I don't usually—"

"Dar?" His gaze grew serious, and he inched closer. We still weren't touching, but I could *feel* the heat from his body. He reached out, once again brushing his finger lightly across my cheek before breaking contact.

The movement was so fleeting that my powers didn't have a chance to respond. "You don't ever need to be embarrassed with me. You're beautiful and sexy as hell. I know a lot of this is new to you, and the fact that I turn you on enough that you did something you've never done before tonight only makes me want you more. Just know that I wouldn't have it any other way. You already know that I love that you're a virgin. I fucking *love* that you've never done stuff like this with another guy." He inched closer, his entire naked body stretched out beside me. "Once we figure out how to get rid of that darkness inside you, I'm going to fuck you until you scream."

My cheeks grew even hotter.

He chuckled. "You're cute when you're embarrassed."

I smothered a smile but pulled the covers over me again. Even though I'd never taken off my clothes, I still felt exposed, and even though Logan made me feel more confident about my sexuality, all of it was uncharted territory for me.

Logan, on the other hand, seemed perfectly at ease in his skin, naked or clothed, and never seemed to be anything but entirely confident and comfortable.

"I wish I could be more like you," I whispered.

He raised an eyebrow. "What do you mean?"

"You're so sure of yourself. You never seem embarrassed, and you can lie right there, completely naked, and not feel the need to cover yourself."

He glanced down at his body. "Do you want me to

cover myself?"

"No!"

He chuckled. "You know part of this is because I'm a shifter, right? When I shift from my wolf form back to human, I'm naked. All werewolves are. It's not unheard of for a group of us to be walking around the woods in nothing but our birthday suits."

"And that's never bothered you?"

He shrugged. "When you grow up that way, it feels normal."

I covered my face with one hand, heat rushing up my cheeks. "I've been modest my whole life. I don't know if that will ever change for me."

His fingers encircled my wrist, and he gently pulled my hand down. I gasped and reared back just as the dark power rushed forward, but Logan broke contact in time.

Still, my heart hammered as I fought to control the power. At least my light stayed calm. As a potential mate, Logan was one of the only people that was the case with.

"You like playing with fire, don't you?" I said shakily.

Regret shone in his gaze. "No, I just hate that I can't touch you. Sometimes, I can't help myself."

"The darkness responded just now, when you did that." I still wrestled with it, but already, it was calming.

"I know. That's why I let go."

"How did you know?"

"A look of panic crossed your face." He raked a hand through his hair, his expression regretful. "I'm sorry. I need to control myself around you more, but it's hard. Wolves like to touch. It's in our nature, and not being able to touch you is driving me crazy."

I swallowed, my heartbeat slowly calming since the dark power had fully retreated. "I know. It's hard for me, too, but Logan, we can't. Not until this power is gone."

# Chapter 17

A dream filled my mind of Logan, wolves, packs, and hierarchy. I clung to it. In the dream, Logan was touching and kissing me. *Yes.*

The bed dipped, making me roll.

"Dar?" Logan's soft question brushed against my ear. I awoke to the feel of the sheet sliding off me.

"Mmm?" I asked sleepily. I opened my eyes to see Logan lying shirtless beside me. The early morning sun peeked around the curtains. The delicious dream vanished, but I smiled lazily. "Good morning."

His eyelids grew hooded. "Morning. How did you sleep?"

"So good." I stretched and yawned. I'd had dreams all night of him. Just the memory of my most recent dream made my cheeks heat and my girly parts tighten.

He inhaled, a knowing look entering his eyes.

"Do we need to get up?" I glanced at the clock. It was just after six.

"Not yet, but I had an idea of something we could try before we leave for the day."

"What?" I turned on my side to face him, my gaze traveling over his broad chest and lean waist. *Damn. So hot...* I could definitely get used to waking up to that.

"I know that I can't touch you right now, but other things can touch you, right?"

I cupped my head in my hand and tried to concentrate, but it was hard. My head was still foggy from sleep. "Things? What do you mean?"

"Clothes. Bed sheets. Backpacks. All of those things touch you and the dark power doesn't react, right?"

I raised my eyebrows and yawned again. "Yeah, you're right. I guess I never thought of that. It's only people that provoke it."

He grinned devilishly. "So that got me thinking . . ." He lifted a long feather from the bed.

My gaze widened as I took in the soft feather in his hand. I then surveyed the small collection of other items by his side—a cup of ice, a long satin ribbon, a soft washcloth, a firm rubber ball, and a few other household things. Someone had obviously been awake for a while.

"I want to touch you even if I can't *directly* touch you." He lifted a strip of cloth.

My lips parted, and all sleepiness vanished. *"Oh,"* I exclaimed. My heart beat faster, my core clenching as I understood what he wanted to do. I squirmed, and the urge to clench my thighs together grew stronger. "Wha"—I cleared my throat and said breathlessly— "What did you have in mind?"

He shifted closer but made sure to keep a few inches of distance between us. "I want to worship your body. I want to make you orgasm, except this time, I want that orgasm to be entirely from *me*." The ring around his irises glowed. "Will you let me?"

I breathed shallowly. "What would I need to do?"

"For starters, you can take your shirt off," he replied in a husky voice.

My eyes bulged, my nipples already hardening in excitement, but— "Just give me a minute." I leaped off the bed and ran out of the room.

In the bathroom, I panted shallowly. I didn't know exactly why I'd just freaked out, but . . . I closed my eyes.

It was *Logan* back there—my overprotective, sexy as sin, unfailingly good and kind boyfriend. I was falling in love with him, and he wanted to pleasure me in the only way he could at the moment. All of that was normal boyfriend and girlfriend behavior. *So why am I panicking?*

I took another moment to use the toilet and brush my teeth. Feeling more alert and refreshed helped. After glancing in the mirror, I fixed my hair then returned to the room.

Logan waited on the bed with an apprehensive expression. "Are you okay?"

"Yeah." And I was. I *wanted* to do this.

I fingered the hem of my shirt then paused. Even though Logan had seen my naked breasts before, I'd never been so casual about getting undressed. The other times had been in the heat of the moment.

"Dar, you're beautiful," Logan whispered, as if reading my mind.

And that, right there, was why I loved him. He always knew how to make everything okay.

After taking a deep breath, I vowed to embrace the new sensuality in my life. *No more hesitation. No more virginal blushing. Dammit, I don't even want to be a virgin anymore.* I wanted the werewolf lying on his bed, looking as sexy as sin, to rip every last ounce of modesty from my soul until I lay bare and wanton in front of him.

I crawled back onto the bed and gripped the hem of my shirt. With one strong pull, I stripped it off. Once it was over my head, I let the cotton top flutter to the floor. My breasts jutted out, proud and defiant—a mirror of how I was determined to feel.

Logan's eyes glowed brighter as his gaze stayed on my boobs while an erection tented his boxers. "Damn woman," he whispered.

Seeing the glow in his eyes made my breath catch. He stared at my tits like a dying man spying an oasis.

"Do you like what you see?" In the cool bedroom air, my nipples budded, growing taut as he drank in the sight of them.

"Yes. Fuck *yes*." He dragged in a breath and shook himself. "Have I told you that you have the most beautiful breasts I've ever seen?"

I bit my lip. "You may have mentioned that."

He inhaled another ragged breath. "This is going to be harder than I thought. It's torture not being able to touch you."

I spied the items he had at his side. "Are you going to use those?"

He nodded. "Lie back," he said hoarsely. "And let me know if the dark power starts responding. If it does, I'll stop, but if it doesn't . . ."

I shivered.

He growled in response.

Wearing only my shorts, I lay back on the warm sheets, but the cool air still made my flesh pebble.

Logan shifted. "I'm going to put this over your eyes so you can concentrate entirely on feeling what I'm doing to you." He lifted the strip of cloth, which I realized he intended to use as a blindfold.

My core tightened more when Logan slipped the blindfold around my face. The world became as dark as ink, but then his warm breath puffed against my neck.

"Can you see me?"

I panted shallowly, anticipation making me restless. "No."

"Good, now just relax." His soft breath tickled my skin. He was close, *so close*, and his breath was so sweet.

My chest rose and fell in shallow pants as something soft trailed down my arm. I gasped more in surprise than anything. Tingles raced up my neck when the soft feather tickled along my collar bone, trailed across my bare chest, and then grazed down my other arm.

I shivered again, not realizing something as simple as a feather could create such a reaction.

Logan shifted, the bed dipping again. He trailed the feather back up, moving in the opposite direction as the feather left a trail of tingles in its path.

"Logan?" I said breathlessly.

"I'm here babe." He inhaled deeply, and I knew he smelled my aroused scent.

Before I could say anything else, the feel of my shorts being tugged off came. "Lift your hips."

I did as he said, and he slowly slid my shorts down. When finished, I heard them land on the floor.

Nothing covered me at the moment.

*Nothing.*

Well, except for the blindfold.

My breath was coming so fast that I thought I would hyperventilate.

"I can smell your arousal." Logan's sharp intake of breath followed. "Spread your legs," he commanded hoarsely.

I did as he said, my legs slowly inching apart over the smooth sheets.

When my sex was entirely exposed, his ragged breathing filled the room. "You have no idea how beautiful you are."

Another dip came in the bed as he shifted lower. When his hot breath puffed against my core, I cried out, arching off the bed. Before I could ask what he was going to do, something hot and wet slid up my slit, rubbing my clit before disappearing.

I bucked. "Logan!"

"Sorry, babe. I just had to taste you."

I quivered, anticipation building in me like a storm. "Please," I whimpered.

He chuckled. "Please what?"

"Touch me." Naked on his bed, cool air continued to

wash over me. Goose bumps pebbled my flesh, but that was nothing compared to the heat building in my core.

"Like this?" he whispered. He shifted again, the bed dipping near my side. Something cold and wet trailed along my chest. I shivered again. "Ice," he whispered.

My nipples hardened into taut buds as Logan trailed the ice down around my areola. Another shiver struck me when he moved to my other tit.

"Cold?"

"No—" I gasped when the ice slid down my stomach. He circled it around my navel, teasing me. "Logan . . ." I squirmed.

"Yeah, babe?"

"I need . . ."

"Would you prefer something hotter?" he asked.

But I didn't have a chance to respond before he slipped the ice down the center of my swollen sex. I cried out again, losing all coherent thought.

But as quickly as that sensation started, it stopped.

"Logan!" I panted.

The bed dipped again then his warm breath blew close to my ear. "Yes?"

"Please," I begged again.

"I like the sound of that."

He moved lower, the mattress dipping as he positioned himself between my legs. I shivered, my entire body quivering uncontrollably in unquenched desire.

"One more taste," he murmured and then his tongue ran up my core, stopping briefly to lap at the swollen nub.

I cried out again, sensations rushing through me just as my dark power stirred. "Logan!" I cried in panic.

"Too much?" he asked.

I nodded tightly.

He growled quietly. "Such a shame. I can't wait to properly taste you."

The heat in my core was growing so much that I made a move to squeeze my legs together, anything to create more friction, but Logan *tsked*.

"That's my job, sweetheart."

Before I could demand more, he rubbed something against my swollen sex, something soft yet firm. I cried out again.

"Do you like that?"

"Yes," I panted. "Yes, please. Don't stop."

He rubbed it against me again, making slow deliberate circles as he varied the friction and pace. I was panting so badly by the time he pulled back that I wanted to scream.

"Logan!" I snarled when the pressure again disappeared.

He chuckled deeply. "I think I could get used to seeing you in this state."

He continued torturing my body, alternating between rubbing my clit and trailing different items across my breasts and limbs. He evoked sensations in me I'd never known existed.

"So wet," he murmured before the mattress dipped between my legs again. "You're dripping, and it's all from me."

"Logan, please. *Please*." I moaned and shifted my legs, feeling so damned restless it was going to make me scream.

"Your scent is making me crazy," he growled before

blowing on my sex again. "I bet every werewolf at headquarters can smell you. I want to bury my cock so deep inside you right now."

*"Yes,"* was all I could manage.

"But this will have to do."

Something firm pressed against my swollen nub again. I bucked then stopped, so anxious he'd pull away if I moved too much.

"Do you like that?"

"Yes!"

"What about this?" He rubbed me again, and my sex sang in glee.

"Yes. Yes. Yes."

He continued rubbing something against my clit, and I arched wildly. "Don't stop!"

Logan picked up his pace, using slow tortuous movements at first but then moving faster and using more pressure. The waves inside me began to build in earnest, rising higher and higher until I thought I was going to burst.

"Cum for me, babe. I want to hear you scream."

He rubbed me more, the friction against my core so hard I lost all sense of place and time. I screamed, my entire body arching off the bed as an orgasm shattered my insides.

"Fuck you're beautiful."

I continued to quiver, my entire body reveling in the earth-shattering orgasm. It seemed to take hours before I descended from the high. When I finally did, I sighed in bliss, and the blindfold lifted.

Logan discarded it. That golden glow still lit his eyes.

It rivaled the morning sun penetrating the curtains.

I fluttered my eyelids as my entire body felt like jelly. I lay on his bed, completely spent, thoroughly loved, and deliciously sated. A grin spread across Logan's face, and I laughed.

"You look very happy with yourself."

He chuckled. "Every man likes to make his woman scream."

I blushed, unable to help it, but at least I wasn't acting like a bashful virgin anymore. "I wish I could touch you in return."

He leaned closer, and before I could stop him, he kissed me on the lips so quickly that the dark power didn't have a chance to rise. "You will. All in good time."

# Chapter 18

It was hard getting out of bed after that experience, but duty called, whether we liked it or not. A cool nip filled the air when we walked outside on our way to the main complex.

My long blond hair whipped in the wind, and when I'd looked in the mirror before leaving, my turquoise eyes had been particularly bright. I figured it had something to do with what Logan and I had done. I smothered a smile, but any lingering romance from our morning had ended as soon as we stepped outside.

Tension emanated from Logan the closer we got to headquarters, his impending meeting with Wes obviously weighing heavily on his mind.

"It's getting colder." I hugged the sweatshirt more

tightly around me. I'd picked jeans to wear since September had arrived with a vengeance. Autumn was definitely on its way.

My statement penetrated the steely resolve surrounding Logan, exactly as I'd hoped it would. He shook himself. "It won't get much colder than this. At least, not in headquarters."

"What do you mean? Doesn't it get cold here in winter?"

"Yeah, outside of the magical barrier, it does, but the sorcerers' magic won't let the temp fall below fifty on our land."

"So no snow then?"

"Nope. Even if there's a blizzard outside the barrier, in here, it's clear and dry."

I was still trying to contemplate the amount of magic that would take when we reached the main doors. A magical scanner emitted pink light around Logan's handprint. A soft robotic voice followed.

"Welcome, Logan Smith and Daria Gresham." The door clicked open.

Nervously, I ran a hand through my hair. "What should I do while you're talking to Wes?"

"I'll have you wait in one of the break rooms. Hopefully, this won't take long."

I followed Logan down a maze of corridors until we reached a room with a few tables, some chairs, and a vending machine. "Help yourself to some coffee." He nodded toward the coffeepot on the counter. "And stay here. For real this time."

He winked, but I still groaned. I definitely wasn't

making *that* mistake again.

Before I could wish him well, he disappeared from the room. To pass the time, I poured myself coffee and checked my phone. I still hadn't talked to Cecile and Mike since arriving, but when I opened my text messaging, I didn't have service.

So I sat down and sipped my cup of hot brew. I had only just finished my cup when Logan and Wes appeared in the doorway.

"We'll proceed to the library now, Daria." Wes opened the door toward a wide hallway. "Master Gregor and Master Mallory have been assigned to this case."

Before I could ask what the heck that meant, Wes turned and went into the hall.

I raised my eyebrows at Logan. "So? What happened?"

"I'm on probation," he replied quietly.

"What does that mean?"

"It means if I fuck up again, I'm out."

My jaw dropped. "You'd get kicked out of the SF?"

"Yeah, for good."

He said it calmly, but I still noticed the tenseness in his shoulders that hadn't been there earlier. If he got kicked out of the SF, he would have to return home, and that meant facing whatever he was running from.

"Come on." He nodded toward the door. "We don't want to keep Wes waiting."

We left the room and hurried to catch up with the SF general as he wove his way down a myriad of corridors. When we approached another wide hallway, my attention focused on the large doors waiting ahead.

"This is the library." Wes waved at the grand entrance.

The monstrous doors rose at least twenty feet high and looked about a thousand years old.

Wes reached for one's handle. "Gregor and Mallory have been poring over old texts and scrolls all morning. I'm hoping they'll explain why those rogues had red eyes, why they were working together, and how you killed them. Perhaps what we find will aid you in understanding how you killed them and, ultimately, help us teach other witches how to harness a similar power. If nothing else, it may help you learn how to control whatever was born inside you, Daria."

"I certainly hope so." I followed him inside, the door creaking open on giant hinges. I jumped when the ancient door slammed closed behind us, but that surprise quickly abated when the library spread out in front of me.

"How in the world . . ." I whispered.

The library rivaled the size of a football stadium and had a ceiling at least a hundred feet high. Rows and rows of shelves, stacked higher than seemed humanly possible, towered all around the room. But it wasn't just the sheer size of the cavernous monstrosity they called a library that shocked me—it was also that the shelves *floated* above the floor.

Dozens of large floating shelves, each thirty feet tall, swayed and moved in the air, as though they had life forces of their own. My gaze flew upward when a particular shelf suddenly shot into the air as one of the higher-up ones plummeted down.

I jumped back, shrieking, but it stopped about five

feet away and floated two feet off the floor.

Logan smiled, apparently finding my reaction amusing. "Magic's pretty cool, eh?"

"You could say that, but how is this room so *big?*" The headquarter building did not look that big from the outside.

"Again, magic." Logan winked.

"Don't worry about the flying furniture," someone said, coming up behind us. "The shelves are just doing what they're told. Mallory and I are still trying to find a scroll from a text I recall reading several hundred years ago."

I turned around to see a figure hunched over, hobbling toward us. He wore an earthy-brown-colored woolen robe that draped over his four-foot body. When he peeked up at me, I swallowed a surprised yelp.

"Daria, this is Master Gregor." Wes waved at the newcomer. "He's our oldest scholar and most experienced historian. When the courts called him yesterday to tell him about your case, he accepted the prisoner's punishment and returned to help."

*Prisoner's punishment? What the heck is he talking about now?* But I didn't have time to ask because Master Gregor hobbled closer to me.

"Daria Gresham, it's a pleasure. I've always wanted to meet a Gresham witch."

"Nice to meet you, too," I somehow managed despite having the urge to ogle. Between the large pointed ears, the elongated snout, the gaping mouth filled with sharp teeth, and the large dark eyes set in a face that looked like stone, I did my best not to flinch. Master Gregor's features were so grotesque that they were the kinds of things children had nightmares about.

"Let me see if what I remember is here." Master Gregor hobbled toward the shelf that had come careening down only a moment before.

Logan, Wes, and I stayed put as Gregor leaped onto a ladder gliding past, the graceful movement belying his unsteady walk.

The ladder ascended to the top of the floating shelf, where Gregor leaned out and began thumbing through ancient-looking books and scrolls.

"What is he?" I asked Logan under my breath.

Logan leaned down and replied quietly, "A gargoyle. Their species is well renowned for their academic achievements."

*Gargoyles are scholars? Not warders of evil? Sure, why not.* "Is that why he looks like stone?"

"Yeah. At night, he turns back to stone, but during the day, gargoyles work in supernatural libraries throughout the world."

"And what did Wes mean about the prisoners and courts?"

"I'll explain that one later."

Guessing that we didn't have much time before Gregor sailed back down, I asked a simpler question. "Where did he travel from? Wes said he returned from somewhere."

Logan scratched his chin. "I think Eastern Europe. The largest supernatural library is in Bulgaria."

"Wow, he must have jumped on the first plane out. That's a long way."

"My guess is he used a portal key. Then it only takes a few minutes to travel anywhere."

My jaw dropped. Logan had told me before that portal keys were precious. Did that mean the SF considered what had happened with the rogue wolves important? That they would whisk a coveted scholar in overnight to get on the case?

Gregor floated down the ladder, holding a scroll. "I think I've found it." His wide mouth with its gray lips stretched into what I could only guess was a gargoyle grin. "Mallory's still in the back wing, hunting through newer texts, but I believe I've found the most important one."

He hopped off the ladder as nimbly as a cat. Once on the floor, he hobbled past us to a large wooden table. "Let me show you."

My heart pounded when I approached the table. If Master Gregor knew something about the dark power inside me, it was possible the scroll he held contained the first clue to explain what had happened to me.

Gregor unwrapped the scroll on the table. Creases lined the ancient paper, but when I peered closer, I saw that it wasn't paper at all but cloth.

Since the text was in a different language, I couldn't read it. "What does it say?"

Wes and Logan also stood behind Gregor, each easily double the small gargoyle's size.

"It says . . . ah, right here!" Gregor said, pointing. He ran his long finger with its curly claw over a particular line of text. "This speaks of a race of witches renowned for their healing power, specifically that they can heal within and without, rendering the sick whole and unsoiled."

"So this is about my family?" My heart beat harder.

Gregor bobbed his head, his finger flying down the text. "It is. At the bottom here, there's a mention of the Gresham witch. Did you know your family originally hailed from the Mediterranean area?"

I fingered my hair—my very *blond* hair. "Really?"

"Indeed. The Greshams only left that area during the Holy Wars, when they became persecuted for their practices."

I bit my lip, nerves churning in my stomach. All of that was news to me. My mom and my nan certainly never knew anything about it. If they had, they would have told me. I was certain of it.

"But what of the power inside her now?" Logan asked, hands on his hips. "What causes it, and why does she have it?"

Gregor leaned down, his large eyes flying over the ancient text. "There's something here at the bottom." He clapped. "Yes, this is it! This is what I remembered! Right here, it says that the Gresham women first emerged around AD 200 and that their power was both dark and light."

My breaths grew shallow, my heart rate increasing more. "Dark and light? We didn't just have light?"

"No, your family had both." Gregor rolled the scroll back up.

"Wait. What are you doing?" I called as he hobbled past us again to the ladder.

"Why, putting this parchment away. It's imperative that we return all texts to their original location. It's the only way we can keep this room organized." He gave me another toothy gargoyle grin.

"But what does the dark power do?" I asked, stepping closer to the floating shelf as Gregor ascended the ladder to the top.

"Why, I have no idea," Gregor replied. He floated back down and hopped nimbly off when he reached the floor.

"Is there anything that talks about other witches being capable of doing what Daria did?" Wes asked.

Gregor shook his head. "Not that I recall. I can ask my colleagues in the various libraries, but neither Mallory nor I recalled reading anything other than what that scroll just revealed."

My heart plummeted. "You mean, that's it? But I thought that you could help me figure out how to stop it."

"Or help her learn how to control it so she can train other witches," Wes added. He didn't look particularly enthused about the new information, either.

Gregor bobbed his head again. "It's possible there are more answers in this library or another, but my task now is to search for answers to explain red-eyed rogues and rogues working in a pack. However, in my free time, I could help you more. Would you like me to see what I can find?"

"Yes! I—"

"No," Logan cut in. "We won't be needing you to do that quite yet."

My mouth parted as I turned his way. "Why not?"

Logan steered me away and said under his breath, "You don't want to make any deals with gargoyles."

"But why? He could help me!"

"And he could end up owning your life in the process."

My eyebrows knit together. "What are you talking about?"

"Have you noticed how old he is? Gregor is easily the court's oldest scholar, but that's not from natural aging. Gargoyles can only come alive and stay alive during the day if they harvest human or supernatural life. They're kind of like leeches. They must feed off others' energy forces to live during the day, and if they don't, they return to stone . . . indefinitely."

"So you're saying that if I ask him to help me further, he'll take my life?"

"Not all of it but part of it. Depending on how much research he does and how extensive his search is, he could shorten your life by days, years, or decades. Right now, we're not that desperate."

I glanced over my shoulder. Gregor and Wes were discussing something. "Then whose energy force has he taken to be helping us right now?"

"Remember your question about the courts and prisoners? Well, if gargoyles practice legally, they only leech life from those sentenced in the supernatural courts. We don't have capital punishment, not like the human world, but we do have punishments that take years from a criminal's life. The gargoyles are deployed for that sentence, but some gargoyles don't play fair, and they leech life without a supernatural knowing."

"And that's what Gregor would have done to me?" I practically screeched.

"No, he practices fairly, so he would have explained it first, but I didn't think you'd fully understand the ramifications of what you'd be agreeing to. That's why I stepped in."

I straightened. "But couldn't Wes ask Gregor to search more? Cause doesn't he want to learn about my power, too, you know, in case other witches could benefit?"

"Yes, Wes is interested, too, but since he hasn't already, I'm assuming that means he can't use any more of Gregor's time without sacrificing something personal. A gargoyle's time is considered very precious. The gargoyles' knowledge supersedes any supernaturals in our world. They're very sought-after. And right now, Master Gregor must be following the court-appointed regimen, which is apparently more focused on the red-eyed rogues versus your family's past."

My shoulders drooped. "So now what? If we can't ask Gregor to find anything else without him taking part of my life, what am I supposed to do? All Gregor found was that my family once had both dark and light powers, but that still doesn't tell me why or what it is, and we still don't know how to get rid of it."

"No," Logan agreed, "but it does tell us that your ancestors once held this power, and *they* were able to get rid of it since no one in your immediate family had it. If they could, then you can too."

A smile grew on my face as his logic took hold. "In other words, we just need to figure out *how* my ancestors got rid of it."

"Exactly."

# Chapter 19

Following our meeting with Gregor, Logan suggested we venture into Boise for a walk around the supernatural marketplace while we tried to work out a plan for what to do.

I couldn't agree more. I needed to clear my head.

Fresh air flew in through the window of a brand-new SUV as we cruised down the road. Since headquarters provided vehicles for all SF members when they were on site, we were in a luxury Mercedes with leather seats and an interactive dash. It was pretty much the exact opposite of the tour bus in every way.

I nibbled my lip as headquarters faded behind us. Trees flashed by my window as the magical barrier loomed ahead. Gregor's findings kept swirling through my mind. *Their power was both dark and light.*

I frowned. *Both dark and light.*

A memory brushed the back of my mind, like butterfly wings flapping on glass. I gasped, the memory slamming to the forefront of my mind.

My jaw dropped. "Logan, do you remember the psychic I told you about? When I almost got bitten by that rattlesnake on that hike we went on? She said this would happen to me."

He cocked his head in my direction, his beautiful dark hair brushing the top of his forehead. At first, confusion filled his eyes, but then they widened in understanding. "The psychic you met at the rest stop when you were a teenager? Is that what you mean?"

"Yes, she told me this would happen." My heart pattered faster. Words from that conversation came back to haunt me.

*"A time will come when you'll feel both the dark and the light."*

I angled my body toward his. "She was right. What she predicted is exactly what's happened to me."

My breaths came faster, and I rubbed my damp palms on my thighs. I'd told Logan about the psychic, just the other week when we lay in the grass on top of a hill overlooking a rest stop. He'd asked me who the most interesting person was that I'd met in my travels around the country. I'd recalled a woman from several years back. She'd approached me when I'd been a sulking teenager in a park and had told me cryptic things.

I grabbed his forearm, not even realizing what I was doing until the dark power stirred. I recoiled, horrified at what I'd done, but my excitement soon took hold again. "Do you think we could find her? If she knew this about me, maybe she would know more, and talking to her wouldn't require giving away any of my life."

Logan nodded, his hand gripping the wheel harder as we sailed around a curve in the road. "We can try. Do you know her name?"

"No."

"How about where she was from? Or lived at that time?"

"No. I don't know anything like that."

"Do you remember what she looked like?"

I perked up. "Yes, she had dark hair and bright-blue eyes."

He gave me a placating smile.

"What? What's wrong?"

"That's how most psychics look. They all hail from the same region in the world, so their coloring is similar. What about a birthmark? Or a tattoo? Or some other unique identifying mark?"

I chewed on my lip, my initial excitement fading more as each mile passed. "No. I don't remember anything like that. It was so long ago."

Logan took a deep breath, that placating smile returning. "We'll still try. I'll look into it when we get back and see what we can find in the database based off what you remember of her appearance."

I nodded and settled back in my seat. I knew it was a long shot, but if we found the psychic who'd predicted what would happen to me, it was possible she could predict more, and with any luck, she would give me a direction to follow so I could finally be rid of the dark power once and for all.

I just had to find her.

∞   ∞   ∞

Half an hour later, we drove along the streets in downtown Boise. Since it was Saturday, foot traffic clogged the sidewalks as people bustled to and from shops, restaurants, and bars.

"Where's the marketplace?" I asked.

"It's hidden right in the heart of downtown Boise. You have to be a supernatural to enter it, similar to getting into headquarters."

"So it's like headquarters, meaning it's in the middle of civilization, yet the humans don't know about it?" For a moment I paused. I'd just referred to humans as if they were a different species. That was a first.

"Yep. Exactly that." Logan pulled into a parking spot off the street then pointed at a Mexican café near the corner. "How about we eat there before heading to the marketplace."

My stomach growled at the thought of food. "Yeah, good idea."

Once parked, we strolled down the street to the restaurant as I peeked around for clues of a magical barrier somewhere in the vicinity. I didn't spot anything. "So where exactly is the supernatural marketplace?"

"The entrance is two blocks ahead. You'll know when we reach it."

When we entered the Mexican café, Logan murmured

something under his breath to the hostess.

She nodded in a conspiring way and grabbed two menus. "Right this way."

I gave Logan a side-eye. "Are you up to something?"

He feigned surprise. "What? Me?"

I was still watching him suspiciously when we rounded the corner, then I spotted two familiar faces. "Cecile! Mike!"

Cecile stood from her chair when we approached, a relieved expression crossing her features. "There you are! I've been worried sick about you!"

More than anything, I wanted to throw my arms around her and wrap her into a hug. The past twenty-four hours had been so tumultuous that seeing the two people in the world that I considered family completely grounded me. But as I rushed forward, the dark power inside me rose. I stopped midstride, nearly tripping, and shoved my hands into my back pockets.

"It's so good to see you both." The very underwhelming statement felt hollow and trite.

"You, too, Dar." Mike smoothed his mustache before sitting back down in his seat. "Cecile's been a little worried about you since we weren't sure when you'd be back."

I pulled back my chair, too, causing the wooden legs to scrape against the tiled floor.

The hostess smiled pleasantly and set our menus on the table. "Your server will be right with you."

When she left, I twirled in my seat to face Logan, who had pulled out the chair beside me. "You planned this, didn't you? You knew I'd love to see them."

He shrugged. "I may have texted them and asked them to meet us here."

"And it's a good thing he did!" Cecile said hotly. "I was really starting to worry. For the life of me, I can't remember you leaving!"

"I'm sorry, Cece. If I could have gotten in touch sooner, I would have."

Cecile shook her head. "I remember you and Logan being in the bus with us and that we planned to part ways when we reached the headquarters, but then everything gets fuzzy. You know me—I like having everything planned, and I like to know exactly what's going on, but I can't remember what we talked about or when we had planned to meet up again."

Mike patted her hand. "I tried to tell her that you're a big girl and capable of taking care of yourself, but she was having none of it." He winked.

I gave Cecile a sympathetic smile. "Logan said that would happen when we approached headquarters. It's the sorcerers' magic. It toys with human memories, so you wouldn't know when we left the bus to enter the portal."

Cecile's eyebrows rose as she picked up her drink. "Are you saying a sorcerer changed my memories?"

I squirmed. "Yes."

She set her drink down calmly—too calmly. "I see. And is that something that will be done to me often? Will my memories often be manipulated without my knowing?"

I took a deep breath, not in the least surprised by her anger. "I'm sorry, Cece, but yes, if you come with me to headquarters often, it will happen every time."

Logan leaned forward. "It's a necessity. If we want to stay safe in the human world, we have to safeguard our privacy. None of us take pleasure in manipulating memories. Please accept my apology on behalf of the SF."

Cecile straightened, some of the irritation leaving her face. "All right, I see. In that case, I may avoid headquarters, if that's all right with you, Daria."

"Or I can show you exactly where the mind-manipulation starts," Logan offered. "That way you can still be near Daria without your thought patterns being disorganized."

Cecile smiled, any trace of annoyance vanishing. "That would be lovely, Logan. Thank you."

I sighed in relief and settled back. We all ordered a mountain of food to share, and the lunch passed quickly.

"So what's the plan now?" Cecile asked when we stood to leave. She slung her purse over her shoulder and pushed her chair back under the table.

"Right now, Logan and I are heading to the supernatural marketplace. We managed to find one answer this morning about the dark power. Apparently, the women in my family used to have it, but at some point, they lost it." *Or buried it.* The feeling of the dark power cracking open inside me, when the rogues had attacked, hinted that it had always been there. I'd just been unaware of it.

Mike cocked his head. "You don't say. How long ago was that?"

"Hundreds of years ago. According to the scholar we spoke with, an ancient text from the dark ages hinted at my family possessing both light and dark powers."

Cecile frowned. "But neither your mother nor your grandmother had any dark powers, and they never mentioned any of their ancestors possessing anything like that, so what happened to it?"

I began walking toward the front of the restaurant, Cecile at my side. "That's what we're trying to figure out. Logan and I are going to try to find a psychic who may know something, but if that doesn't work, we'll ask the scholars for more help, but that comes with a price."

Cecile's eyebrows rose. "A price?"

"You don't want to know. Trust me."

My statement, not surprisingly, only made her frown deepen.

"Are you still planning to stay at headquarters for a few more days?" Cecile asked when we reached the restaurant's entryway.

"Yeah, as long as I don't get kicked out." Priscilla's and Chloe's faces flashed through my mind along with Phoenix's. I hoped his injuries were healing. "Since I can't heal clients while I have this dark power inside me, I'll need to keep searching for a way to get rid of it." *Or learn to control it.*

Ever since waking in the healing center the previous night, it had stayed in my mind that the dark power had healed me. Its power was vastly greater than my healing light. And since it had healed me unaided . . .

*Maybe it's not entirely bad.*

But until I understood it, I had no way of harnessing it or trying to use it on anybody else.

"So now what?" Cecile asked as she and Mike stepped

through the front door. The sunshine streamed through the boulevard trees lining the sidewalk.

My shoulders slumped. "Now, we part ways again."

Mike sighed. "I figured as much." He pulled out his phone and tapped on a tourist app. "Should we see what there is to do in the area, Cece?"

Cecile's lips tightened into a thin line, her fingers curling around her purse strap until her knuckles turned white. "Just be careful, okay, Dar?"

I felt Logan drift to my side, his tantalizing scent carrying in the wind. I shuffled closer to him, wishing I could lean against him and take comfort in his warm presence. "I will. I promise."

We said our goodbyes with all of us agreeing to talk soon. A moment later, Logan and I were striding down the block toward the supernatural marketplace. The sun shone as we skipped around people mingling on the sidewalk.

I was so deep in thought, trying to remember details about the psychic, that I almost walked right past the magical barrier.

"Oh!" I exclaimed when the glowing red rope-like tendril appeared near an alleyway. I sniffed and detected the subtle scent of mint and anise.

"We're here." Logan hooked a thumb toward the barrier.

"You don't say."

His lips quirked up.

We stood on the sidewalk, by an alleyway in between two shops. On the right was a bakery. On the left, a mom-and-pop's hardware store. Heavenly scents drifted

Power in Darkness

from the bakery, and mouth-watering pastries lined the shelves in its window display cases. I licked my lips. Apparently, my stomach had forgotten that I'd just gorged on margaritas and a boatload of tacos.

"So how do we get to the marketplace?" I peered into the dim alleyway. It couldn't be wider than ten feet, a thin ribbon of sky above.

"It's at the end, off to the right. The entrance is similar to headquarters, only you don't need clearance. Any amount of supernatural blood will gain you admittance."

Excitement pumped through my veins. "Lead the way."

Logan's muscled forearm brushed against mine when he stepped into the alleyway. It was so brief that I didn't think he was aware of it.

Still, his touch affected *me*. I paused to admire the dip between his shoulder blades and the sexy swagger of his hips. An ache formed in my core again, memories of the previous night assaulting me.

"Is there something you'd like to share?" He glanced over his shoulder, a knowing smirk tilting his lips up.

Heat rose in my cheeks. "No, I . . . uh . . ." I rolled my eyes, embarrassment following. "I keep forgetting you can smell my arousal."

He inhaled, the rings around his irises lighting up. "You smell like a rose bud ripening just for me."

A lightbulb clicked on, making me pause midstride. "Roses in heat. So that's what you meant."

He stopped too. Ahead, the magical barrier grew brighter. "What was that?"

"That's what you said the other week, right before you left in Miles City on the Greyhound. You said I smell like roses in heat."

Understanding lit his eyes, his lips curving up more. "Oh, right. Yeah, that's what I was referring to."

I stepped closer to him. Two feet separated us, and my fingers ached to reach over and lace themselves through his. I opened my mouth to say as much, when Logan's nostrils flared.

"Do you smell that?" he asked.

"What? My roses? Or the donuts from the bakery?"

"No, it smells like—"

Two men walked around the corner, both tall, lean, and pale.

Logan's lip curled. "Vampires."

# Chapter 20

A sardonic smile lifted one of the vampires' lips. His pale-blond hair looked almost white. "Well, hello, Major Smith. Is the SF monitoring the supernatural marketplace now? Afraid someone's going to steal granny's spiced apples or a fairy's going to bite someone?"

The other vampire, a dark-haired one, snickered.

Logan bristled when they approached, his hands clenching into fists. "What are you two up to?"

"Oh, not much," the blond replied. "Just checking out the new potions for sale, and we thought we'd maybe grab a cape or two. The modern look just doesn't suit us like the Dark Ages did."

The dark-haired one laughed again at his sidekick's sarcastic reply.

The blond vampire paused at my side, leaning closer. He inhaled, his nostrils flaring. "My, don't you smell sweet!" He inched closer.

The dark power rushed up, making me leap back.

Logan shoved the vampire away. A deep growl tore from his throat, and his voice lowered to that strange cadence as dominant power rushed out of him, filling the alleyway and making goose bumps erupt on my skin. "Keep your distance. I wouldn't want to make a scene."

The vampire's eyes widened, but he quickly recovered, smoothing back his slick blond hair before eyeing my boyfriend icily. "Now, now. No need to go all alpha on us. I was simply inhaling that delicious scent of hers. I can't say I've ever smelled anything like it."

I nearly rolled my eyes. "Let me guess. Roses?"

The vampire cocked his head, eyeing me as the sun glistened off his hair. "Roses and something else—"

"Wait a minute," I cut him off. "You're in the sunlight. How are you not dead?"

"Dead?" the blond one asked.

The vampires glanced at one another, the dark-haired one beginning to grin. "From sunlight?" They both burst into laughter.

The dark-haired one turned a devilish grin on me. "You're Daria Gresham, aren't you? The healing witch who's only just been introduced to the community? The one who knows nothing about our ways?"

I shuffled my feet uncomfortably as the dark power swirled inside me. "Um, yeah. How did you know?"

He stepped closer, getting a warning growl from Logan.

"Oh, relax." He *tsked* in Logan's direction, shaking his head. "I merely wanted to do this—" He lifted my hair and turned it in the sunshine.

The dark power rushed upward, and I flinched back, breaking contact.

The vampire didn't seem to notice. "Long blond hair, small build, turquoise eyes, and . . ." His gaze drifted to my chest, where my breasts strained against my shirt. His eyes darkened, his tongue darting out to lick his lips. "And oh so *delectable.*"

Logan's hand shot out, wrapping around the vampire's neck. He pinned him against the alleyway building, his muscles bulging when he lifted the vampire a few inches off the ground.

The other vampire sighed in exasperation.

Logan ignored him, keeping his attention on the blond-haired one. "Like I said earlier, keep your distance, blood sucker, and don't get any ideas. She's taken." He lowered him to the ground.

Logan relaxed his grip, and the vampire carefully pried Logan's hand loose doing it finger by finger, a grimace on his face.

"Really, Major Smith. You wolves are so possessive and territorial. You should loosen up, spread around the fun." He rubbed his throat, but already the bruises Logan had inflicted were fading. "Besides, I bet she's as hot on the inside as she is on the outside." His hand strayed to his crotch. "I'm getting hard just thinking about it."

The dark-haired vampire grabbed his friend out of the way just as Logan lunged for him.

"He meant no disrespect," he said, hauling his friend

away.

"Sure I did." The blond one laughed. He swiveled his gaze to me again. "See you around, beautiful."

The two vampires sauntered out to the street, turning the corner into the bright sunshine, leaving me standing there, mouth agape. "What the hell just happened?"

Logan still seethed. "Nothing that's uncommon around blood suckers. I fucking *hate* vampires."

"Are they all like that?" I asked, stepping closer to Logan. The dark power swirled inside me, once again letting me know it was available. *Not now!* I pushed it down, as if it were a poorly behaved dog, and thankfully, it stayed there.

"No, not all of them. Just most of them." He rolled his shoulders, the tension still evident in them.

I smiled, unable to help it as I took in Logan's demeanor. "It's almost like you're my bodyguard again, jumping in to stop anyone from getting too close."

Logan ran an agitated hand through his hair. "If you'd been able to smell his arousal, you'd have been angry too." He swung my way, his dark gaze traveling over my face and body. "If I hadn't been around, he probably would have influenced you to go back to his place, even though that's illegal. I don't even want to think about what you would have done with him."

"Influenced? Does that, like, manipulate your mind or something?"

"Exactly. It's what vampires can do, even to supernaturals."

"So why didn't he influence *you?*"

"Other than it being illegal and meaning he'd end up

in an SF holding cell? He can't. Everyone in the SF takes a daily potion to prevent influencing from happening. Speaking of which, I should start giving you a dose every morning too."

"So without that potion, and without you here to stop what he wanted to do with me, I could be . . . right now—" I pictured the vampires both on me at once, biting me, kissing me, fucking me, doing things to me that I'd never done with any man, but then I laughed. "I wonder what the dark power would have done to them."

Some of the frown lines on Logan's face smoothed, an amused grin lifting his lips. "Maybe next time we should find out."

We both laughed before carrying on down the alleyway.

"Why did the vampires think it was funny when I asked why they weren't dead?" I asked.

"It's an old wives' tale that vampires burn in the sun. They tolerate sunshine just fine. Unfortunately."

"So they don't sleep in coffins or crypts during the day?"

His lips quirked up as we approached a glimmering portal door. "No. Most likely, they sleep on Egyptian cotton sheets in luxury apartment buildings at *night*. Vampires are known for their extravagance. They usually prefer flashy cars and designer clothes, and monogamy is not a word they're familiar with."

"So they sleep around a lot? Don't they catch diseases or get a lot of STDs then?"

"Our kind isn't prone to human diseases. You're not, either."

"I'm not?" I stepped closer to the glowing red portal, the hint of mint and anise much stronger since the door loomed so close. My interest in learning more about vampires waned given what stood in front of me. "Good to know. So is this going to be as bad as the portal into the headquarters?"

"Not quite as bad. There aren't security checks here like there are there. The journey is much quicker, and we can go together." He made a move to grab my hand but stopped at the last moment, regret filling his face. "Or not."

I eyed his hand longingly. "I'll see you on the other side." Before I could lose my nerve, I stepped forward.

As soon as I jumped through the glowing door, I plummeted through space, squeezing, twisting, and popping all at once. But just as quickly as those sensations started, they stopped.

Still, the brief journey was jarring. Panting, I straightened when I finally felt secure enough to stand on steady ground and not tip over. I surveyed what lay in front of me. Before I could blink, Logan stood at my side.

"And here it is. The supernatural marketplace." He gestured ahead.

I grinned as I took in the busy streets churning with activity. We stood at the end of a cobblestone lane, the glowing portal door right behind us. Someone bumped into Logan as he made his way to the portal.

"Excuse me, mate." An Australian accent lilted his words.

Logan and I moved aside as the man jumped through a portal to the right from which we'd come. He disappeared instantly.

"There's more than one portal?" I asked, eyeing the multiple glowing red doors.

"Yeah, those portals all lead to different areas of the world. Do you want to look around?"

"Is that a rhetorical question?"

He chuckled and began to wander down the narrow cobblestone street, and I followed like an eager puppy, lapping it all up.

Lining both sides of the street were old-fashioned-looking vendor tents with canvas awnings covering their wares. Large tables with a mixture of food, glass bottles filled with colorful liquids, weapons of various sizes and shapes, games, strange things hanging from racks, and other knickknacks and paraphernalia covered each table's display. It was an endless supernatural wonder.

At each vendor tent, supernaturals stood behind their tables, peddling goods and eagerly making sales.

A fairy off to the left had rows of earrings studded through her pointy ears. Curly purple hair trailed down her back as she enticed a customer with powdery goods she held out in her hand.

The customer dipped his finger into the powder before tasting it. He nodded and pulled money from his pocket.

"How are things paid for here?" I asked, darting to the side as a group of kids raced around us.

They laughed and carried what looked like large lollipops. However, the lollipops sparkled and cracked, as if alive in their own way. *Maybe not lollipops but instead magical fireworks?*

"We use the same currency as the outside." Logan gestured to an old woman. She looked like a human, so I guessed that she was a witch. She appeared to be selling, funnily enough, spiced apples.

Another supernatural, a woman with long black hair, piercing blue eyes, and translucent skin, took the bag.

"Siren," Logan said under his breath, gesturing toward the woman with the black hair.

"She's a mermaid?" I asked in awe, looking for her tail. Obviously, she didn't have one on land, but my gaze still trailed down her slim legs, which were clad in shorts. An abundance of her pearly, shiny skin was on clear display.

"Mermaid is another word for them," Logan replied.

The old witch held out her hand before the young siren deposited a twenty-dollar bill into it.

"Initially, we had our own currency," Logan continued, clasping his hands behind his back as we strolled down the street. "But it proved to be too much trouble since we've integrated so closely into the human world. Now"—he shrugged—"we just use the same money."

"Is it US currency?"

"All currency is accepted. It's easy enough to trade the money at a bank in whatever country you normally reside in. And because the supernaturals in the world are the minority, we tend to ignore country borders. You'll find a lot of people from around the world here. Portals make travel easy for us."

The grin didn't leave my face as we wandered from street to street. The supernatural marketplace was much larger than I'd anticipated. Row after row of cobblestone streets intersected every which way. Just when I thought the end was near, Logan would steer me in another direction, and we would suddenly be standing at the beginning of another long row of shops and vendors.

"Do you want to buy anything?" he asked as rich, fragrant scents of something stewing in a pot tickled my nose. If not for the tacos, I would have asked for a cup.

I grinned eagerly but then remembered my financial state. "I didn't bring much money, so I'll just look."

Logan gave me one of those looks that I was coming to learn meant he didn't approve of my answer. "What would you like? I'd be happy to buy it for you."

"Logan," I replied in a firm voice, "you're not responsible for me. You don't have to buy me things. I'm fine with just looking."

"Really?" His dark eyebrows rose, his square jaw tilting my way. "I saw the way your eyes lit up at the necklace back there. The one with the onyx pendant hanging from the silver chain?"

I shrugged. "The color reminded me of your eyes at night."

He reached into his pocket and pulled out a silver chain, dangling it in front of me. I gasped when the beautiful smooth onyx pendant caught the light. But then I stuttered, "But h-how did you get that?"

"I might have bought it when you turned your back to look at those bracelets."

A warm feeling slid through me as he reached behind my neck to clasp it in place. He was careful to avoid touching me, but I still felt his heat. It sent delicious shivers down my spine.

He leaned closer, still careful, but an air of intimacy flared between us. "Every time you look at that, I want you to think of me."

I brought my hand to my throat and felt the smooth stone beneath my palm. "Thanks, and I will. I love it."

He kissed me on the neck before I could pull back, but once again, he moved so fast that the dark power didn't have time to respond.

"You're getting quite good at those quick touches."

"Not good enough." His expression turned regretful. "It's hard for me to pull back. I'd rather stay."

"I'd rather you stay too." The words came out breathy as my stomach flipped. Hastily taking a step away, I returned my attention to the marketplace. "Is there anything we haven't seen?"

He gestured to the end of the lane. "There are a few more vendors back that way. Do you want to see them?"

We began walking that way, careful to avoid the crowds that mingled near some of the shops. So far, I hadn't brushed against anybody or made contact with anyone. Since it was midday, I guessed that most people were at work or school, similar to the human world.

We were just about to round the corner to the last row of shops when the sound of jingling bells reached my ears. I paused, that faint sound making the hairs on the back of my neck stand on end.

I turned around, searching for the source. Off to the right, behind a shop lined with Oriental-looking carpets, a woman disappeared. Bells jingled around her ankles, and long black hair swayed against her butt before she disappeared from view.

My heart pounded, and my body drifted toward her as if on its own accord.

Logan cocked his head, but stayed put, buzzing from his pocket drawing his attention. He pulled out his phone to check a text.

I ducked behind the hanging carpet, the rough texture brushing against my fingers. In the dim room behind it waited a table and chairs. The woman stood near the corner, her back to me.

I stepped closer, my breathing coming so fast that I felt lightheaded. *It's her! I know it's her!*

"The young Gresham woman has found us at last." She stayed turned away, but her words were crystal clear when they drifted toward me.

"It *is* you! You're the psychic from the park!"

She swung around to face me. Her smile revealed a crooked front tooth, but it didn't distract from her beauty. Porcelain skin sheathed her face, jet black hair tumbled down her back, and eyes so blue they sparkled like the ocean regarded me steadily. "And here you stand, having felt both the dark and the light, just as I predicted."

I grinned as I stared at the psychic I'd encountered in my teen years. "But you *knew*. How did you know?"

The woman laughed, the sound as musical as the bells that jingled around her ankles. "Because I'm a psychic, sweet child. That's what I do."

"Did you know I was coming today?"

"Of course."

I rushed forward. "What else do you know? Do you

know where my dark power comes from? Do you know how I can get rid of it?"

The woman placed her palm against my cheek. I flinched back, but her hand stayed put. As if sensing the dark power rise inside me, she pulled away in time.

"To find the answers to your future, you must look into your past."

I groaned in frustration. "I already know that. I already know that my family once possessed both of these powers, but how do I get rid of the dark one?"

The psychic reached behind her to a pad of paper sitting on a table then picked up an elegant-looking pen with a feather attached to the top. She wrote something down before ripping the paper off and handing it to me.

"I won't charge you this time, but next time, it will be a different story. This is someone who may be able to help you, but he's not . . ." She tapped the feather against her cheek. "As *worldly* as the one standing outside waiting for you."

*Worldly? Is that another cryptic message?*

I took the paper she held in her outstretched hand. It held three simple words.

*Daniel. Vendor 109.*

# Chapter 21

My lips parted just as a rush of air fluttered over my cheeks. I looked up to see one of the rugs swaying.

The psychic was gone. I pulled the rug back, searching frantically for where she'd disappeared to, but behind the rug was a narrow alleyway. Doors lined the alleyway every few feet.

She was nowhere to be seen, obviously having gone into one of the doors. I sighed in frustration. Once again, she'd entered my life and left it as mysteriously as she'd come.

Despite being disappointed that I couldn't ask more questions, excitement still rose within me. Giddy, I burst from the small room behind the carpets and ran back to the street.

"Logan! Logan, where are you?" I frantically searched for my boyfriend and spotted his head above a sea of people a few vendors down. A grin still lit my face as I ran toward him.

"Logan! I found—"

I stopped short when the crowd parted.

Draped around my boyfriend stood a tall, beautiful girl. Long, wavy brown hair flowed down her back, and her lithe body pressed against Logan's side. She had one arm entwined around his neck, the other trailing familiarly up and down his stomach. Her fingers moved along his abs confidently, as if they'd traveled that path before.

My lungs seized, and my heart felt as if it had stopped.

Beside the beauty, Logan wore an uncomfortable expression. He reached behind him to grasp the young woman's wrists before gently trying to push her away. She pouted prettily and kept her hold on him, murmuring something in his ear.

As if sensing me, Logan's head snapped in my direction. Guilt flooded his gaze as confusion and hurt welled up inside me, prickling my gift.

*Surely I'm seeing things.*

"Logan?" I asked, my voice wavering. I staggered toward him, not knowing if I should approach.

The beauty raked her gaze up and down my frame.

"So this is her." She propped a hand on her hip. Her long red nails flashed in the sunshine. "I've heard about you, how you've been trying to sink your little claws into something that doesn't belong to you."

Pain entered Logan's eyes. "Daria, I need to talk to

you."

"What's going on?" I asked, my feet rooting to the ground.

The girl laughed, the sound brittle yet amused. Goose bumps erupted along my skin. I wrapped my arms around myself as the dark power flared coldly.

"He really didn't tell you?"

Despite Logan trying to push her away, the woman remained at his side, her arm snaking around his waist. Hot jealousy coursed through me.

"I'm Crystal. Logan's fiancée. Did he forget to mention that little detail?"

My jaw dropped, my fingers curling around the paper in my hand. Only two minutes before, I'd been filled with joy and hope at finding answers just around the corner...

My eyes found Logan's again. I didn't want to believe Crystal. I'd trusted Logan. He'd told me he didn't have a girlfriend. He'd told me that he was available.

*But did he?*

With lightning speed, I recounted the numerous discussions we'd had. He'd only ever told me that he didn't have a *girlfriend.* He'd never actually told me who Crystal was other than a girl back home.

So was this one of his *responsibilities* he was avoiding at home?

Hysterical laughter bubbled up inside me. "So is that how it works? You tell me you don't have a girlfriend because she's really your *fiancée?* Is that what honesty means to you, Logan? Semantics?"

Logan's face fell. He pushed Crystal off him and stepped closer to me, his arm reaching out. "Daria, please. I can explain."

The hysterical laughter finally escaped my lips, the sound shrill and sharp. "So it's true? She's your *fiancée?*"

Crystal stepped forward, tossing her long dark hair over her shoulder. She stared at me with accusing green eyes. "Do you really think you're the first woman who's tried to steal him away from me? Logan's quite the catch, as I'm sure you know. Women are always trying to get him, but we've been promised to each other since we were kids. He's meant to be with *me*, not *you.*"

"Crystal," Logan said through gritted teeth. "Back off."

She barely gave him a glance before turning her attention back to me. "You didn't think that you were really going to end up with him, did you?"

Logan's hands clenched into fists, and he shot her an angry glare. He took another step closer to me. "Daria, let's talk, please. Let's go somewhere alone where I can explain." He held his hand out, his large palm open, just waiting for me to grasp it.

But I couldn't. Even if I wanted to touch him, I couldn't.

*I'll never want to touch him now.*

I spun away, my breath trapped in my throat. I couldn't breathe. I couldn't think. I couldn't move. Pain coursed through me in such intense intervals that action was impossible.

*Move, Dar! Just get out of here! Get away from them!*

Crystal laughed, the sound as hauntingly beautiful as she was.

That laugh jolted my limbs into action. I took off

through the crowd, her laughter following me. That laugh conveyed that I'd been played for a fool, and everyone was in on the joke except for me.

I sprinted down the street, clutching the paper to me as if my life depended on it, which it very well could have.

"Daria!" Logan shouted, but I darted around the corner onto another street before blindly running to the end.

I zigzagged through the marketplace, not watching where I was going, running into people as I ran in a blinding fury. The dark power swirled and filled my body, creating a tremendous sense of power along my limbs.

*I have to get out of here. I have to find the portal!*

But as that singular thought entered my mind, the paper clutched in my hand caught my attention. *Daniel. Vendor 109.*

I stopped midstride, panting, as other supernaturals looked at me curiously from where they stood and shopped. I could only imagine the spectacle I was making of myself, but my brain felt like it was going to explode.

*Daniel. Vendor 109.*

I twirled around in a circle, searching for numbers. *There!* Tiny numbers lay etched into the stone at the foot of each vendor's table. The booths were numbered, just like a city street in the human world.

Nearly tripping, I stumbled to the nearest shop. "Where's one-oh-nine?"

The fairy behind the table raised his blue eyebrows. "Excuse me?"

I held up the paper, showing him what the psychic had written. "Where's vendor one hundred nine?"

He nodded down the street just as Logan shouted my name in the distance, but I couldn't talk to him. I couldn't face him. He'd lied to me. He'd lied through his teeth about who Crystal was.

*What did he think? That telling me she wasn't his girlfriend would somehow annul him of any responsibility to her? That word play would mean he hadn't lied?*

I took off in the direction the fairy had nodded at, trying to pay attention to the tiny numbers as I whizzed past each shop.

When I rounded another corner, my gaze darted to the ground. *106. 107. 108.*

I careened to a stop, nearly pitching over, in front of the vendor with the tiny cobblestone reading *109*.

The simple booth held a display of various knickknacks that rivaled a touristy shop in the human world. Little children's toys, cheap-looking baubles, and tacky jewelry lined the table. The man behind it eyed me curiously. "Can I interest you in anything?"

I took a step forward, adrenaline making my hand shake. "Daniel. Vendor one hundred nine."

Part of me expected him to look at me like I was crazy. That was how I felt. Inside, I was falling apart and unraveling at the seams.

But instead of waving me off, his curious smile disappeared, and a new reverence lit his eyes. "Right this way."

He stood and pulled back a curtain draped behind him, revealing another dimly lit room behind the outdoor shop, similar to the psychic's booth.

Logan again shouted my name. Except it was louder

and closer.

"Hurry. I don't have much time." I dodged around the vendor's table. I couldn't let Logan find me. I didn't want to talk to him or even face him. Pain shot through me in such intense intervals. He'd *betrayed* me.

The man dipped his head. "As you wish."

I entered the space behind the curtain, and he gestured toward the corner. "It's there."

I peered into the dim corner. "What's there?"

"Daniel."

"He is?"

"Why, yes. He's right in there."

I squinted. Something wavered in the air. Subtle purple colors shimmered in the shape of a . . .

My forehead scrunched. *A door?*

An undercurrent of powerful energy prickled my skin. I took a step closer. Something lay in that corner, something powerful and magical.

My feet tapped lightly on the stone floor, each step bringing me closer to whatever powerful magic filled the man's shop.

The hairs on my arms stood on end as the dark power buzzed to life inside me, rushing up and wanting out, excitement making it strong.

"What is that?" I asked warily.

"Daniel."

It didn't seem that the shopkeeper would be giving me any answers.

*"Daria? Daria!"* Logan's frantic yells grew louder, more anxious with every call. His werewolf senses meant he could easily track me. I probably only had seconds

before he found me.

Before I could think better of it, I lunged forward, right toward the shimmery purple energy.

The curtain behind me ripped open, and Logan leaped into the room.

But the purple energy had already encompassed me, syphoning me into its embrace as the dark power and my healing light sang with glee.

Logan's eyes grew wide, his mouth opening with horror, but the world around me disappeared, as if fading to black.

Logan's fear-filled eyes were the last things I saw before everything went dark.

# Chapter 22

The feeling of being ripped apart and torn to pieces from the inside out made me scream. If I had thought traveling through the headquarters and marketplace portals were bad, they didn't hold a candle to the purple portal.

The sensations grew and grew, until it felt as if my heart was going to burst. I screamed again, but it carried no sound. Wherever I was, senses from the human world held no meaning.

*I'm going to die. I'm certainly going to die.*

But just when I felt for certain that my life would end, the sensations stopped. I landed hard on something solid, my legs buckling beneath me as harsh pants emitted from my mouth. I fell forward, grabbing for something to hold onto, anything tangible that I could grasp.

My fingers sank into something spongy. Whatever I'd landed on was solid, but also . . . not.

Airy, white fog drifted around me, the whiteness stretching farther than I could see. I tentatively peered around while my heart slammed against my ribs.

Panting, I called, "Hello?" My voice sounded small, fear threatening to suffocate me. I squeezed my eyes tightly shut. *What have I done?*

I could feel that I was no longer on earth. I was somewhere else, somewhere unknown. My dark and light powers buzzed inside me, as if rejoicing.

But then the hot, searing pain of Logan's betrayal came back. *How could he do that to me?*

"What have we here?"

I snapped my head up, searching for the bearer of that voice. Off to the side stood a man. No, he wasn't a man. He was something else, something *other*.

"Daniel?"

He drifted to my side, his movements graceful and languid. His skin held a subtle glow, and his features were so beautiful that they rivaled anything Michelangelo had painted. But when my eyes met his, I hissed in a breath.

Irises an identical shade of turquoise to mine stared back at me.

"Who are you?" I searched for answers on his inhumanly beautiful face. An ethereal quality surrounded him, making my powers sing. I slowly rose on the spongy ground.

With every second that passed, my dark and light powers billowed, feeling calm and serene as if they were . . . *at home.*

The turquoise-eyed man smiled. "I'm Daniel. And you are?"

"Daria Gresham."

Never had my powers felt as they were. Normally, my light sat just below my navel, where I always tried to bury it—control it—but in the strange world I'd come to it swelled to my skin, pulsing and pushing, until a billowy light filled the air around me.

"Strange," Daniel muttered. "You glow like us, and I can sense something in you that is like me, but it's different." He cocked his head, his perfectly sculpted eyebrows drawing together. "What are you?"

I scoffed. "What am *I?* What are *you?*"

"I told you. I am Daniel."

"Right, but *what* are you?" He had to be at least six-three, and he had broad shoulders, wavy dark hair, and turquoise eyes that bore a startling resemblance to mine.

My heart continued to pound. I took another step closer to him and tried to calm my breathing. The air felt different, thicker but lighter at the same time. It was too bizarre for me to comprehend.

"What do you mean, Daria Gresham?" An amused smile lit his face. "I'm what you are."

Ignoring my frustration at getting sucked in a conversation of riddles, I stepped even closer to him. "Daniel, can you help me? Can you help me figure out what's going on inside me?"

His beautiful face stretched into a grin that was so breathtaking that for a moment, everything inside me stopped.

I stood in the presence of pure beauty that was

unrivaled in the human world.

My mouth grew dry as I soaked up the energy of his presence. Looking down, I muffled a yelp when I saw my arms. Similar to Daniel's, my skin glowed.

"What help do you need?" he asked, his tone still slightly amused.

I let my arms fall, and my breath started to come faster. *I'm glowing. I'm freakin' glowing!*

I didn't even want to consider where I was or how I would get back home. Just the thought of how impulsively I'd stepped into whatever portal lived in vendor 109's tent made me want to cry with worry.

*Get it together, Dar! Remember why you did this!*

I cleared my throat then said, "I have this power that was born inside me. It's too strong. I can't control it. I need help getting rid of it."

"Power inside you?" He cocked his head again. "Of course you have power inside you. That's what we're made of."

*"We?"* I took another step closer to him. The glows around our skin touched and mingled. For some strangely alluring reason, I wanted to be even closer to him. "What do you mean, *'we'*?"

That curious and amused expression filled his face again. "Why, I do believe you're the most curious angel I've ever met."

"Angel?" My mouth went dry, and my feet planted.

He laughed. "Isn't that what you are? It's what I am, and I can see that you're one of us." He tapped a beautiful, elegant finger on his chin. "Different, yes, but still one of us. Now, shall we talk about why you're here?

I haven't had a visitor as curious as you in over a millennium."

I cradled my head in my hands, my long blond hair running through my fingers as I tried to understand what he was telling me. "But how do you know that I'm an angel? I thought I was a witch."

"As I said previously, you're different from other angels, but I can sense your power, and the glow of your skin signifies your divine status, but . . ." He tapped his chiseled chin again. "Something inside you isn't quite right."

"What do you mean?"

"Your powers. They feel . . . off."

"Is that because I'm really a witch? Maybe you're wrong about me being an angel."

"Oh no. I'm not wrong, although you may be part witch, but you are most definitely an angel."

For a moment, I just stood there while Daniel, who was apparently a pure-blooded angel, towered above me. Being beside him made my inner dark and light powers feel calm and at home. Both flowed languidly and free through my body.

They'd never felt that way before.

I bit my lip, frowning. On earth, my light always stayed stored in the chest below my navel that I'd created as a little girl, but not free. *Never* free. When my light ran through my body, it was too painful. So I only called it forth for a healing session . . . or it escaped if someone touched me. But at least I knew what my light was—it was to heal others. As for the dark power, I still didn't understand *what* it was or *why* it had been born inside me.

Extending my arm, I studied the satiny glow. Just beneath my skin's surface, energy prickled and flowed serenely yet powerfully, my dark and light powers *both* coursing through my body.

*So what the heck does that mean?*

I shook my head, glancing up at Daniel again. He wore a curious expression as he stared down at me.

"But how is it possible that I'm an angel? I live on earth."

Daniel elegantly lowered himself to the ground, his muscled thighs pressing through his bright-white pants as he crisscrossed his legs. "Would you like to sit with me?"

I fell to the ground in a heap. Unlike me, he'd somehow made the movement appear fluid and graceful.

He cocked his head. "So you live on earth? My, that *is* peculiar."

"So you really don't know anything about me? You don't know who I am or how I'm an angel?"

"No, I don't, but perhaps I could help you learn the answers to your questions."

"Could you? Oh, please. Yes! Whatever you're able to tell me would be fantastic."

The white fog descended more around us, caressing my skin like air on a humid summer night. Strangely enough, the temperature felt warm and comfortable, even though clouds on earth only lived high in the atmosphere, where the temperature plummeted.

I angled my body to face Daniel more and settled into the spongy ground. "But first of all, can you tell me where I am? I'm guessing I'm no longer on earth, considering I'm sitting in the middle of clouds on something that doesn't quite feel like the ground."

Daniel's shoulders sagged. "You're correct. You're no longer on earth, but most unfortunately, you're not in heaven, either."

"Heaven?"

"No, we are currently residing in Emunda."

I cocked an eyebrow. "Is that supposed to mean something?"

That amused expression lit his ethereal face again. "For an angel, you're quite uneducated."

Suppressing an eye roll, I said, "Well, in my defense, until about ten minutes ago, I didn't know I was an angel."

"True. Very true. In that case, since you are ignorant of what Emunda is, I shall enlighten you." He spread his arms wide. "Welcome to the land of lost angels, a land for those cast from the gates of heaven. My fellow divine beings who reside in this realm have been deemed unworthy of our maker's heavenly grace at this time. However, we are still blessed enough to not be cast into the gates of hell, so this is where our maker put us."

"Our maker? As in God?"

Laughter lit his turquoise eyes. "You could say that."

For a moment, my heart stopped. "So does that mean I'm stuck here now too?"

"Oh, no. Nobody is *stuck* here. This is just where we reside when we're not allowed in the heavenly realm, but it does not mean we cannot depart. There are many options for whence we could travel. Is there one in particular that interests you?"

"You mean other than earth?"

Daniel clasped his hands loosely in his lap and rested his elbows on his knees, drawing my attention to his shoulders. His rounded muscles pressed against his white shirt, and in a way, his lean, strong build reminded me of Logan.

I sucked in a breath, the pain threatening to suffocate me. *Logan.* I squeezed my eyes tightly shut. Logan was engaged to Crystal. He had a fiancée. Technically, that meant he was no longer my boyfriend. Our relationship had ended as quickly as it had begun.

"What ails you, my young angel?" Daniel's amused smile vanished, worry in his tone.

I forced a smile, pushing the pain down. "Nothing. Just something I was running away from on earth."

"So perhaps earth isn't where you would like to reside. Would you like to visit the fae lands? They're quite beautiful, especially this time of year."

"Fae lands? Is that where the fairies come from?"

He smiled again, the beauty of his face taking my breath away. Another twinkle sparkled in his eyes. "For an angel, even one that came to fruition on earth, you're quite uneducated on multiple levels. Are you really suggesting that you didn't know of the fae lands?"

"No, I didn't know." I ducked my head as my cheeks heated. "A month ago, I thought I was the only supernatural on earth. Since then, I've been enlightened that I'm one of tens of thousands of supernaturals, and that's just in the United States. Apparently, there are even more worldwide, and there I was, thinking I was a special snowflake, when really I was just one of the masses."

He tilted his head. "But you *are* special. An angel

living amongst the humans and supernaturals . . . I can't say I've heard of that before."

"You haven't? But I'm not a full angel, right? Cause honestly, I always thought I was a witch, and you said I'm not exactly like you but something different." I held up my arm again. "And look at our skin. Yours glows more, and you're"—I waved at his face—"you know, ridiculously good looking. Is that an angel thing?"

An amused smile tilted his lips up again. "Angels are known for being *ridiculously good looking*. Speaking of which, you're quite beautiful as well."

My cheeks heated. "But as you said, I'm not quite like you. So what am I?"

His head cocked to the side. "Well, you are part angel—that is for certain. As for what else you are…" Daniel shrugged. "Only your mother can tell you."

My breath hitched before I forced my lungs to expand. "I would ask her, except my mother is dead."

# Chapter 23

Daniel's eyes dimmed. "I'm sorry to hear that. I did not know."

"It's okay. How could you? We just met."

We sat in silence for a moment on the spongy surface. The misty trails of clouds swirling around us lifted. My breath sucked in when I spied waterfalls, light-pink mountains, and fields so beautiful I stopped breathing in the distance, but then the fog descended again cutting off my view.

"So what do I do now?" I asked. "I came here to find answers. A psychic told me to look for Daniel and that you could help me. And she was right. I've found you, and you've given me some very meaningful answers. I'm grateful for that—don't get me wrong—but what now?

Every time I find another answer to explain what's going on with me, I find more questions that leave me even more confused."

"What are you confused about?"

"According to you, I'm part angel, but according to my mother and the people I met in the supernatural community, I'm a witch. So what does that make me? Part witch and part angel? Is that what a *supernatural healer* is?"

His eyebrows drew together as a pensive expression grew on his face. "You could be part witch. You are undeniably an angel, even if you're not a full-blooded one. Otherwise, the Emunda portal would not have accepted you. And if your witch ancestry was confirmed as you suggest, then perhaps that's also true."

"I wouldn't be here if I weren't an angel?"

"Oh heavens, no. Only angels are allowed in Emunda. Angel blood is required to activate the portal transfer from whence you came."

"So part witch and part angel. Hmm . . ." My thoughts drifted back to when I'd first entered the Supernatural Force's headquarters. Millie, one of the fairies employed by the SF, had scanned my wrist. The SF's technology had identified me as a witch, but their scan hadn't picked up my angel blood. Perhaps that was because normally, angels didn't walk on the earth—as Daniel had said—so the SF didn't have a means of identifying them.

"So does my angel side explain my dark and light powers?"

Daniel cocked his head. "The powers inside you? The

dark and the light, as you say? Yes, those are angel powers."

"And are your powers dark and light too?"

Daniel leaned back on the spongy, opaque ground, as if settling in for a long chat. That delightful smile curved his lips up again. "If you're speaking of the power inside us that makes us what we are, yes, it is dark and light." He arched a perfectly sculpted eyebrow. "Does that also mean that you are uneducated on *what* our powers are?"

I frowned. "Um, kind of. I've always had my light, but I've only recently discovered my dark." I explained as succinctly as possible the incident with the rogue werewolves. "It was that encounter that awoke my dark power. I killed them with it." I shuddered, remembering the evil force swirling inside the rogues and how I'd blasted the dark power from my palms into them, stopping their hearts. "And I didn't just kill them. The power that shot from me was red, not gold like my healing light, and it basically turned them into gelatinous goo. They were a bit hard to clean up." I winced. I hated thinking about that incident.

"Gelatinous goo?" A chuckle escaped Daniel. "I haven't heard another angel describe a reckoning quite like that, but I suppose that's an accurate term."

"A reckoning?"

"It's what we call it when evil is banished or destroyed." When I just stared at him blankly, he added, "It's what we were created for. Well, *part* of what we were created for. We carry divine power that thwarts evil and destroys it when necessary, but we can also foster life and heal. What you just described was your dark angel power activating as it was intended."

"You mean my dark power killed them because they were evil?"

"From the sounds of it, those rogue werewolves were entirely evil, so yes, that's exactly what happened."

"But why did I not know of my dark power before then? Why did an encounter with three nasty rogues bring it out? I've encountered evil people before." An image of Dillon, my biological father, flashed through my mind.

"All angels recognize pure evil when presented with it. How do you say it on earth . . ." He tapped his chin, then his eyes lit up. "Ah yes, it is like an internal *sensor*. Our powers rush forth when evil awaits. As for why you didn't know of your dark power before then"—he shrugged—"I know not."

"Do you know how I can get rid of my dark power? So I only have my light again?"

Daniel jerked his head back, a shocked expression crossing his face. "Why in the heavenly realms would you want to destroy part of your angel powers?"

"Because I don't know how to live with the dark. I can't touch anybody—not that I ever could before—but it's so much worse now. Every time I get anxious or afraid, the dark power comes rushing forward. I very nearly killed Phoenix—an innocent supernatural back on earth—and I almost accidentally killed my boyfriend several times." I paused and took a deep breath. Just thinking of Logan made an unbearable ache rise in my chest. "Well, ex-boyfriend now."

"I don't like seeing that sad face of yours, young angel."

I shook myself out of my melancholy and faced Daniel squarely again. "You might be able to live with both of your powers just fine, but I don't know how to. I need to either banish my dark power back to where it came from or I need to learn how to control it. I can't go around potentially killing innocent people because I don't know how to handle my angel powers."

I frowned. *Did I really just refer to my powers as angel powers?*

Funny how quickly I was coming to accept it. Perhaps it was because the past few weeks had been one eye-opening experience after another.

"Dearest, Daria, dare I ask what you're thinking?" Daniel's turquoise eyes glittered with delight.

"Nothing. But back to the matter at hand, can you help me? Do you know how I can get rid of my dark power?"

Daniel shuddered, his sculpted shoulders shivering beneath his loosely flowing top. "I would never help another angel rid themselves of their power. I am fairly certain I would never be allowed to enter the gates of Heaven again if I were to commence such an atrocious offense. However, if I were to help a young angel in distress, such as you, perhaps that would put me in a more divine light with our maker."

"Okay, I have no idea what you just said there, but does that mean you're going to help me?"

Daniel chuckled, his eyes twinkling once again. "Why, yes, Daria Gresham. It would be my pleasure to assist you."

"Great!" I jumped to my feet, readying myself for

whatever was to come. "So what do we do? Do you touch me and instill me with your vast knowledge and ability to control my powers? Or do you show me how to push it down when it tries to rush up? Just tell me what to do, and I'll do it."

He pushed himself up, coming so gracefully to his feet that he reminded me of a cat stretching in the sun. "Heavens no. We shall do nothing like that. However, I will train you. Based on what you've shared, I suppose you are somewhat similar to our newly appointed angels. When they come into their powers, they are also somewhat confused and show a lack of basic training."

"Really?" I grinned. "You'll train me."

"I suppose so. I'm not exactly busy at the moment."

"All right, so what do I do?"

Daniel opened his mouth but then cocked his head. He stepped away from me, as if listening to something in the distance.

I craned my neck, straining to detect whatever he heard, but all I heard was . . . nothing.

"Did you hear something?"

A grim expression settled on Daniel's face. "It seems there is some trouble on earth regarding you."

"Trouble on earth? How do you know that?"

"I was just given a message. Would you like to see what I'm talking about?"

Unease tingled up my spine. "Is everything okay?" My thoughts immediately drifted to Cecile and Mike. I slapped a hand to my forehead. "Oh crap, are Cecile and Mike looking for me? Are they worried?"

"Well, someone is *definitely* looking for you, but I

don't think it is these Cecile or Mike people you speak of." Daniel waved his hand in the clouds.

The cloud dispersed, as if he'd pushed aside a curtain to reveal a window-like view. I gasped.

Through the makeshift window I could see my boyfriend, correction *ex-boyfriend*, pacing up and down the length of a room within the Supernatural Force's headquarters. My heart beat harder. Just seeing Logan made my stomach flip.

Even though the view didn't have sound, I gathered Logan was yelling. Thick veins in his neck strained, fiery red tinted his cheeks, and the way he constantly flexed and unflexed his hands led me to believe he was royally pissed off.

My heart jumped into my throat, but that was quickly doused when a stinging sense of betrayal hit me. I wondered if Logan had just returned to the SF with Crystal following our supernatural marketplace excursion.

"Do you know this person?"

"That's Logan Smith."

As much as I didn't want to care anymore, as much as I wanted to look away and not be bothered by the sight of him, I would only be lying to myself if I pretended seeing him didn't affect me.

My heart thumped so wildly I could barely breathe, and my powers sparked to life beneath my skin. My body's reaction to him had always bordered on extreme, angel powers or not.

"Is he okay?" I asked, even though I internally kicked myself for caring. "He looks really upset."

Daniel laughed. "Upset? That is accurate if slightly

understated. I haven't seen a werewolf this *upset*, as you say, in quite some time."

"You know that he's a werewolf?"

"Of course. Don't you?"

That time I *did* roll my eyes. "Of course I know that he's a werewolf. He's my ex-boyfriend."

"Well, perhaps that explains his anger. I've been informed that your absence on earth has created a few dilemmas. I've been instructed to return you from whence you came."

"But what about teaching me how to control my powers? How am I supposed to not kill anybody if I don't know how to keep my dark power under control?"

"Why, I shall join you. We shall return to earth, and to this"—he waved his hand toward the image of Logan storming about the room—"this ex-boyfriend werewolf of yours, and from there, we shall commence your training."

"Really? You'll come with me?"

Daniel chuckled again. "Why do I have a feeling that training you will prove to be more amusing than anything?"

"I don't know how amusing I'll be, but I'm really happy that I'll learn to live with this power, or suppress it, or whatever you want me to do." My gaze drifted to the window again, my excitement over being trained by Daniel dimming. I wasn't sure how I was going to face Logan again, and I didn't want to watch him marry Crystal.

"Shall we go?" Daniel held out his elbow for me.

I slipped my hand through the crook of his arm,

briefly realizing that his touch didn't activate my gift, before I stepped to his side. "Yeah. I'll follow you."

# Continue the Story

*Dragons in Fire*, book three in the
Supernatural Community series.

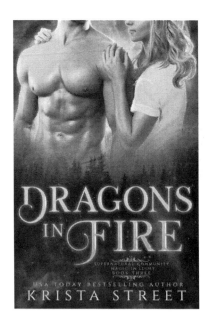

www.kristastreet.com

Thank you for reading *Power in Darkness*, book two in the Supernatural Community series!

If you enjoy Krista Street's writing, make sure you join her newsletter at **www.kristastreet.com** to stay up-to-date on new releases, book deals, and all of the writing stuff she's up to.

And if you enjoyed *Power in Darkness*, please consider logging onto Amazon to post a review. Authors rely heavily on readers reviewing their work. Even one sentence helps a lot. Thank you so much if you do!

♥

To learn more about Krista's other books and series, visit her website. Links to all of her books, along with links to her social media platforms, are available on every page.

www.kristastreet.com

# About the Author

Krista Street is a Minnesota native but has lived throughout the U.S. and in another country or two. She loves to travel, read, and spend time in the great outdoors. When not writing, Krista is either spending time with her family, sipping a cup of tea, or enjoying the hidden gems of beauty that Minnesota has to offer.

Printed in Great Britain
by Amazon

36996515R00151